RESERV

LIVI MICHAEL is an award-winning writer of novels for adults, young adults and children. Her short stories have been published in several magazines and anthologies. She was educated at the University of Leeds and teaches Creative Writing at Manchester Metropolitan University.

LIVI MICHAEL

RESERVOIR

SALT

CROMER

PUBLISHED BY SALT PUBLISHING 2023

2 4 6 8 10 9 7 5 3 1

First published in Great Britain in 2023 by
Salt Publishing Ltd
12 Norwich Road, Cromer, Norfolk NR27 0AX United Kingdom

www.saltpublishing.com

Salt Publishing Limited Reg. No. 5293401

A CIP catalogue record for this book is available from the British Library

ISBN 978 1 78463 290 8 (Paperback edition)
ISBN 978 1 78463 291 5 (Electronic edition)

Typeset in Neacademia by Salt Publishing

Printed and bound in Great Britain by Clays Ltd, Elcograf S.p.A

RESERVOIR

THE WILD BEGAN where the gardens ended.

In the gardens they could name the plants and animals, privet, rose, squirrels, magpies, cats, but in the Wild, there were alien insects, small, furred creatures clinging to the undersides of leaves, droppings from animals they never saw. And a mass of foliage, spotted, striped or mottled.

Everything was tangled, variegated. So many shades of green: the lime green of new leaves or moss, the dark, polished green of holly or laurel, grey-green splotches of fungus.

Together they skidded and slithered down the rough paths towards the place where they were not supposed to go: the stagnant water, the trailing reeds.

Their eyes burned like the eyes of animals on the scent of prey. They were wood-elves, or savages with spears, they wore garlands and flourished green boughs, their clothes flapped around them like animal skins.

Sometimes they lay on the ground, panting, squinting at a dazzle of sun through a net of leaves. The leaves were quivering, edged with fire, and beyond them, the sky was a burning, infinite blue.

As she lay there, breathing it in, her mind became empty and still. She was free.

But that was then.
That was before.

SOMEWHERE IN THE universe an asteroid struck the surface of a planet, a meteorite plunged into a methane sea, and at the International Conference Centre in Geneva, Hannah Rossier came face to face with Neville Weir.

'Annie Price!' he exclaimed, his eyes widening.

Every vertebra of her spine stiffened.

'Hannah,' she said. 'Rossier.'

Neville's eyes widened further. 'You changed your name?'

'No!' she said, a little too vehemently. 'My name was always Hannah. And I married.'

'Oh, so,' he began, and at the same time, she said, 'It was just the children – at school – calling me Annie.'

Neville's gaze grew complicit with understanding. 'Of course,' he said, 'and I was always Weirdo. For obvious reasons.' He smiled deprecatingly, then his eyes widened again. 'But – Hannah Rossier? Professor Rossier? You're the speaker?'

She dipped her head in acknowledgement. *Why?* she was thinking. *Why him? Why now?*

'But you're the whole reason I came to the conference!' Neville exclaimed. His expression had changed to one she couldn't quite name. Almost predatory.

'Really?' she said, discouragingly.

'Your paper, on the neuroscience of empathy – extraordinary.'

She looked across the atrium, for someone, anyone, she

knew. With a rush of relief she saw the clipped, silver head of Jopi de Groot. It was turned away from Hannah and only visible because Jopi was half a head taller than anyone else, but still someone she could claim.

'. . . set off a whole new train of thought—' Neville was saying.

'If you'll excuse me,' Hannah said, stepping away from him, 'there's someone – I have to . . .'

'Oh, of course,' Neville said. 'But how extraordinary that we should meet up here, like this – are you staying here too? In the hotel?'

Hannah could feel her cheeks tightening, her smile becoming fixed.

'I tell you what,' Neville said, 'there's a lovely little bistro here on the roof – do you know it?'

But Hannah was walking away. 'I have to go,' she said, over her shoulder. She should have added something like 'See you soon', but she was already out of earshot. She could still feel his gaze on her as she retreated, but she had to navigate through all the people in the atrium, who had collected by some unseen chemistry into molecular clusters of threes and fours, or larger groups moving with a tidal rhythm.

She could no longer see Jopi's silver head. She had lost her in all these people, she had lost herself. Hannah stood for a moment, bewildered by the acoustic hum of so many voices, so much glass and light. She turned slowly, uncertainly, in a little space on her own. Until suddenly, there she was, Jopi, her friend, who had organised this conference, slicing through the crowds with her head lowered. She wore a linen suit in white and grey, flowing out at the sides like wings. Only as she reached Hannah did she look up, with a smile of startling ugliness: bad teeth, crooked jaw.

'*Ma cherie!*' she exclaimed, always less formal than the Swiss. She held her arms wide.

'Jopi,' Hannah mumbled, submitting to the embrace. '*Ça va?*'

Jopi introduced her to the centre manager, Isabelle, who had a narrow face and emphatic features. She nodded at Hannah then spoke to Jopi so rapidly that Hannah's French, even after all these years, wasn't quite up to it. 'Ah,' Jopi said to Hannah, as Isabelle left, 'complaints, already! What would we do without them?'

Then there were two students, *Bonjour, bonjour!* Volunteers who would help the conference run smoothly, provide water, check the sound. They looked so alike Hannah knew she would confuse their names. Jopi gave her a programme and showed her to the main lecture theatre, an enormous circle with a domed ceiling where the seminars and plenary sessions would take place.

'Impressive, no?' Jopi said. 'This is where all our funding goes these days.'

Hannah remembered to smile. *Neville*, she was thinking. He was so much bigger than she recalled. Obviously, she hadn't seen him since they were children, but the Neville Hannah remembered had been skinny and undersized. Following the girls around because the boys wanted nothing to do with him. The girls didn't either but they were less likely to beat him up. Now he seemed massive – not overly tall, but very broad. She remembered his sideways movement, crab-like, when she had given her name, and shuddered.

'Are you well?' Jopi said, face creased like a pug's with concern.

Hannah said it was nothing, a headache, she had aspirin in her room.

One of the students – François, was it? Pierre? – offered to take her through the glass tunnel that connected the conference centre to the hotel, but Hannah declined.

'But you'll join us for dinner?' Jopi said. 'You haven't seen the restaurant yet – it's spectacular!'

'Of course,' Hannah said, nodding vigorously. She would join them for dinner, in the Restaurant du Lac, at eight.

Only when she was in the lift (which was transparent, so she was hardly out of sight), did she search through the programme.

She had to read it twice before finding his name. There it was, in small print. His lecture was the day before hers: 'Sense and Censorship: the Psycho-Politics of Narrative'.

What did that mean?

There was nothing else, no details. There must be an abstract somewhere, but Hannah was so used to these conferences that she'd barely looked at the materials they'd sent her online.

Preoccupied, she almost forgot her floor, hurrying out hastily before the doors closed. Then she stood baffled by the long corridor with its marbled, shiny floor, its identical doors.

But she was booked into room 422, her card key told her. Which, as it turned out, was near the lift.

How could it be, she thought, sliding the card-key into its slot, that the two of them, from the same small town, the same under-achieving school, had ended up in the same professional field? She'd not seen Neville since primary school. He'd passed the 11+, she remembered, which was unusual enough for their area, and would have gone to the boys' grammar school, but she, almost uniquely in the history of Rosehill Primary, had gained a scholarship to the private grammar. Their paths had never crossed again.

Until now.

The hotel room was painted in a shade that in England might be called *soft olive*, soothing, unobtrusive. The window looked over the lake and there was a bouquet of green flowers, some kind of orchid, euphorbia, hypericum, on the sill. They seemed cunningly designed to look artificial but were in fact real. Otherwise the room was impersonal, a desk for a laptop, a wifi code near the sill. Everything was automated, operated by her card.

Blades of light sliced through the window-blind onto the bed. Hannah sat down on it, looking at the programme again. There, on the back was his biography, Dr Neville Weir from Nottingham University. He'd written a book about language development, *Authoring the Child*. Not out yet – which was why she hadn't heard of it, presumably.

She tapped his name into her phone. And then a thought came to her that set tiny pulses hammering in her forehead. Surely Neville would have done the same.

He would have looked the main speaker up.

He must have known who she was.

III

ALL AFTERNOON, HANNAH remained in her room. She tried investigating Neville, but curiously, there was not much to find. There was an FB account, no longer active, but which seemed to suggest a wife and two sons. His LinkedIn was out of date, there was nothing on Twitter. Apart from his book, he'd written an article, *The Pathology of Shame*, but she could only access the abstract.

An understanding of pathological shame is critical for assessing the psychological effects of developmental trauma . . .

Nothing ground-breaking there. It was hardly enough to get him invited to an international conference like this. Although Jopi did sometimes invite people who were not well known. She liked to think she was boosting people's careers.

Was that why Neville was here? Evidently, she wouldn't find out from his online profile. She would find out, she supposed, in person. Face to face. Unless she spent the entire three days avoiding him.

Or went home.

On impulse she phoned her husband. He would come for her if she asked him, although they lived nearly three hours away in Lucerne. She would say she wasn't well, offer to leave her PowerPoint presentation with Jopi.

She rang him twice but it went straight to voice-mail. *Thibaut Rossier n'est pas disponible en ce moment.*

She wondered if he'd taken his students out for drinks

- something he would only do in Hannah's absence, because he knew she would disapprove. The bill would be enormous, equivalent to the Gross National Debt of some minor country.

Pointless to argue that with him. He loved his students, and they adored him. They kept him young, he told her. Whenever the subject of his retirement came up he would say, *Je suis trop jeune.*

He was 63.

They had met in Switzerland, at a conference like this one. He was not a psychotherapist, but a chemist, researching therapeutic drugs. They had married eleven years ago, when she was 40 and he was 52. They had no children. Hannah didn't want them. In the course of her career, she'd seen enough of what parenting could do. Thibaut had one son, Christophe, from his first marriage. Hannah had assumed he wouldn't want any more, at his age.

When they'd married, and she'd moved to Lucerne, she'd felt as though her real life could finally begin. As though until then, she'd been frozen in suspension. Marriage was like tying the loose ends of herself into a different whole. But now she saw how quickly that could unravel.

Hannah's forehead crumpled as she held onto her phone. But it was ridiculous. What did she imagine would happen? What could Neville possibly say, or do?

She should stop thinking about him.

She put the phone away then stripped off her outer clothing. In her underwear and camisole she began an exercise routine, stretching, breathing deeply, taking her attention to the soles of her feet, the base of her spine.

Time passed with an artificial slowness. Hannah had spoken at many conferences, stayed in innumerable hotels. She was

familiar with the languor of hotel rooms, which she attribute
to their unfamiliarity, the absence of known objects. It was as
though the ordinary trappings of furniture and books wove
her into a temporal frame.

Normally the anonymity soothed her, but now she felt out
of alignment, unfocused. There was discomfort, not a pain
exactly, beneath her ribs. She went through her lecture until
she could no longer concentrate. At some point she realised
she was seeing it through *his* eyes.

What would he think of it?

Would he pick her up on that point?

What questions was he likely to ask?

She imagined him in the lecture theatre, sitting in front of
her. Whichever way she looked, he was there.

Again she rang Thibaut; he was still unavailable.

'Thibaut,' she said. 'Can you call me, please?'

Her voice had cracked a little, which she hadn't intended.
'I'm fine,' she added. 'I'll be going to dinner at eight. If you
get this before then – just – give me a ring.'

Was that better?

What would she say?

Suddenly cross with herself, she tucked her phone into
her bag. It was a little before seven. She had a shower, and
changed into the other suit she'd packed. It was blue-grey,
almost identical to the navy one she would wear for the lectures. Over the years, she'd perfected a minimal wardrobe for
short conferences, two suits, four tops, nightwear, one set of
casual clothes. Because it was evening, she wore a silky top
in pewter with the blue-grey suit, sandals with a tiny strip of
glitter, and earrings. She applied very slightly more make-up.

Then she looked at herself in the mirror.

Her mouth was set in a thin, strawberry-coloured line,

her eyes were greenish, veiled. Her hair was too severe. She pulled a strand of it forwards, realised the strand was grey, tucked it back.

She'd read all the style magazines, had her colours done, knew her shape. Oddly, whatever she did, she always looked the same. Not like Jopi, who had the gift of transforming herself with little touches, an exotic pendant, a flamboyant scarf. Last year, she'd opened the conference in a slinky evening dress that should have looked incongruous but didn't. Everyone had admired her. *Jolie laide*, that was what the French called it.

What was Hannah? *Fade*.

It remained a mystery to her that Thibaut had singled her out, when he had all those admiring students.

You were so quiet, so discrète, he'd said.

Like a secretary?

A little like a secretary.

That's why you wanted me? Because I looked like a secretary?

No, he'd said, *because I thought you'd be wild in bed.*

Usually that memory made her smile, but not now. When she practised her smile in the mirror, her eyes gave her away. Somewhere behind the mascara, she was still Annie Price, that frightened child.

She would enter the restaurant by the side door. If Neville was there she would just leave. She could always eat in her room.

She should be a few minutes late, so she could see him before he saw her.

It would take her nine minutes, she estimated, to walk from her room to the restaurant, which was on the lower ground floor. So she should set off just after eight. There was a little more than half an hour to wait.

She sat down on the bed again, resisting the urge to call Thibaut one more time.

IV

THE RESTAURANT WAS packed. It was impossible to work out who was sitting where. Hannah managed to identify Jopi by her laugh, coarsened by innumerable cigarettes, but she couldn't tell who was with her. So she kept walking, shoulders back, smile taut.

Jopi rose in greeting. 'Hannah!' she exclaimed. 'Over here!' She wore a peacock blue jumpsuit, with a brilliant pink jacket. Her hair was waxed into short spikes. Hannah almost stumbled over the trailing strap of some woman's handbag, and was forced to look down. *Pardon*.

'Here we all are,' Jopi said, as Hannah advanced towards them, slowly, it seemed, so slowly. Finally she managed to scan the other faces and allowed her smile to become warm.

'This is Professor Rossier, our main speaker,' Jopi said, 'and this is Karl Hartmann, from Frankfurt,' a tall, ginger-haired man rose smiling, 'and Heidi Kruse, from Denmark.'

Hannah registered their lightning assessments of her, the interest in Karl's eyes fading. She'd reached that age when only women gave her those appraising looks, evaluating mainly what she wore. And of course, she did the same, automatically, instantaneously. Heidi had steel-rimmed glasses and a sharp smile. She wore a multi-coloured woollen suit that looked as though she might have knitted it herself.

'Isabelle, you know.' Isabelle half rose, smiling, until Hannah waved her down again. She wore stretch leather jeggings, a loose paisley top and pointed leopard-skin mules.

Hannah eased herself into her seat. 'This is nice,' she said, nodding towards the window where the lake lay like a plate of light.

'Isn't it? And yet Isabelle was just telling us that she's planning to move.'

'Really?' said Hannah.

'Only to Annecy. I will still work here.'

Jopi poured wine into Hannah's glass. 'So you will join the commuters from across the border.'

'Exactly. It's so much cheaper. And Annecy is really pretty.'

'But I thought Lucy worked in Besançon?' Heidi said.

'Lucy works everywhere,' Isabelle replied. She turned to Hannah, adding, 'She curates art exhibitions in different cities – Lyons, Nice. My apartment, and her apartment, are full of boxes. Boxes, boxes! We can never find anything. Only last week, her son came to stay, and her mother visited, and I had left the wrong box out, and they put this CD in the computer for him and it was that bizarre woman who operates on herself – you know – Odile. I came in just as she was about to slice off her own nipples with a razor, and Lucy's maman said, "Are you sure this is *Little House on the Prairie?*"'

Jopi cried aloud, Karl laughed, and Heidi said, 'I don't think we should give that kind of art a platform – it's too similar to what some of our clients do to themselves.'

'Oh but art and mutilation are two sides of the same coin,' Jopi said. 'Don't you think, Hannah?'

Hannah took a piece of bread from the basket and said that anthropologically that was certainly true, many tribal peoples self-mutilated.

'Exactly – that is what art *is* – you take one thing and deform it into something else.'

'*Transform*,' said Isabelle, but Jopi ignored her. 'It's in the human genome,' she said. 'It's what we do.'

'I think there are less painful ways of transforming oneself,' said Karl. 'Take a course – move house.'

'Ah, but then you only take yourself with you,' Jopi said.

Heidi said she'd had enough of moving. For years she used to drive between Denmark and Sweden. Now she'd settled in Helsinki, only a short walk from the university. Karl said he loved to travel, he'd recently spent a year in New York and was going to try for another fellowship. He smiled at Hannah. 'What about you?' he said. 'Have you moved around much?'

'A little.'

'Do you have any favourite cities?'

'Tokyo,' she replied to general exclamations of interest.

'What was that like?'

'Did you live there?'

'Did you like it?'

'I loved it,' Hannah said.

'Now there,' said Karl, 'One would truly have a chance to change oneself – become someone different – don't you think?'

'Are we ordering food?' Hannah said to Jopi.

'Certainly we are,' said Jopi. 'I'm starving!'

There was a protracted discussion about the relative virtues of *La Chasse* and *Filet de Perche*. Jopi said they should have something they could all share, and Karl suggested *Fondue Bourguignonne*, but Jopi said that Hannah didn't eat meat and everyone looked at her.

'It's fine,' she said. 'I'm happy to order for myself.'

Heidi said, 'Well, what about raclette – and the asparagus, perhaps?'

Hannah had given up telling people she didn't eat cheese either, there was hardly any point being vegan here.

After some negotiation, during which Karl and Heidi decided to share a side dish of chicken livers, it was agreed they would all have raclette. Jopi called the waiter over to place their order. 'And *wine*! Lots of it,' she said.

The talk moved on to their hotel rooms, too warm, no view. Hannah looked out, towards the lake. There was a shimmer of colour in it, an effect like shot silk. Then she thought she heard her phone, and reached for her bag, feeling a twinge in her hip as she bent to the side.

There was a bump, then a scuffling noise and a clatter.

'Oh, I'm so sorry,' Neville said. 'No, no – you must let me pay for that.'

Hannah straightened slowly.

'I'm so clumsy,' Neville said, dismayed. Behind him a woman was brushing her jacket.

'Like the proverbial bull,' he said, helping her to straighten it, and there was a little fuss of apology and conciliation, before he turned towards Jopi. 'Do you mind if I join you?' he asked.

'Of course!' Jopi said. 'See, the chair is already waiting! Everyone, this is Neville Weir, our psychopathology expert.'

'Hardly that,' Neville said, manoeuvring himself awkwardly into the chair between Isabelle and Heidi. He directed a small smile at Hannah.

'I hope you're happy with raclette,' Heidi said. 'We've just ordered.'

'My goodness, yes!' Neville said. 'I love raclette.'

'There should be enough for everyone,' said Karl. 'But we've ordered chicken livers as a side.'

'Ah, I don't eat meat,' Neville said.

'Another one!' said Jopi. 'You English and your scruples! Anyone would think you hadn't invented the hunt!'

'I'm afraid we don't do much hunting where I come from,' said Neville.

'Yes, Jopi,' said Isabelle, 'You are guilty of cultural stereotyping!'

'Well, but there are only two English people at our table and neither of them eat meat. It smacks of guilt to me. Neville, this is Professor Rossier, your fellow abstainer.'

'We're old friends,' said Neville, warmly.

'Really?' said Jopi.

Hannah couldn't look at him. She picked up the piece of bread on her plate and broke it, once, twice, as Neville launched himself into the tale of how he'd booked the conference specifically to hear Professor Rossier speak, and then, it turned out, they were from the same small town in the north of England, the same small primary school.

There were exclamations of surprise and delight.

'That's so sweet!' said Heidi. 'You came all the way here for your schoolfriend!'

'Oh, I didn't even know!' Neville said, and Hannah glanced at him sharply. He seemed manifestly open, naïve. 'Of course, she wasn't Professor Rossier then,' he said.

'Not at primary school!' Isabelle joked.

'What a wonderful surprise!' said Jopi. 'You travel all the way from New Zealand and meet your childhood friend!'

'I *know*!' Neville said.

Hannah said, 'You've come from New Zealand?'

'Auckland,' said Neville.

Heidi said, 'Now *that's* a long way . . .' and at the same time Hannah said, 'I thought you were at Nottingham?'

And instantly realised he would know she'd looked him up. Neville ducked his head in acknowledgment. 'I was - until earlier this year. But I was offered this post, and really - I couldn't refuse. New Zealand is one of those countries I've always wanted to visit.'

'Me too!' said Karl, but Heidi said, 'Still - it's a long way to come for a conference.'

'Oh, I'd booked the conference well in advance,' Neville said. 'Couldn't resist - anything organised by Jopi here - and of course, I was particularly interested in Professor Rossier's paper.'

He smiled at her with his yellow teeth.

Hannah could hardly leave - she'd already walked away from Jopi once, pleading a headache. She poured herself more wine, gazing steadily at the glass and said, 'Well, I hope it lives up to your expectations.'

'So do I!' exclaimed Neville. 'Or I'll be claiming my money back!' He laughed loudly, and everyone laughed with him, but Heidi said, 'Didn't the university pay for you?'

'Oh no,' Neville said. 'I booked it myself. So I definitely want my money's worth.'

He was still looking at Hannah, she could feel it, although she wouldn't look back. She was furious with him, with herself. Her heart was pounding.

'So tell me,' Karl said, leaning forward, 'New Zealand - is it wonderful?'

'It really is,' said Neville, pouring wine. 'It's everything I'd hoped it would be, and then some.'

They were interrupted by the arrival of the raclette. A waiter brought a small brazier to the table to heat the cheese, and more waiters followed, bringing potatoes, gherkins, plates. Karl turned to Neville.

'You know, I once drove across Canada,' he said, 'and checked myself into a motel near Ottawa, quite by chance - no pre-booking - and the - what do you call it - hotelier?'

'Proprietor?' suggested Neville.

'Exactly – the proprietor turned out to be my first girl-friend! She'd married a Canadian and moved to Ontario. They were running the hotel together!'

After that, everyone had a story of remarkable meetings.

'That's the beauty of travel,' Neville said. 'Wherever you go, you meet someone, or something from home.' He wasn't looking at Hannah.

'You might as well stay where you are!' Jopi joked.

Without appearing to, Hannah observed Neville. It was one of the tricks she'd learned in her profession, along with controlling even the minor muscles of her face. His manner was bluff and hale, but beneath that she detected something different: cramped, as though forced to grow without light.

He reminded her of one of those stores she'd seen in re-productions of nineteenth-century mid-western towns. False fronts made them seem large and expansive on the outside, but inside everything was constricted and cluttered, dark.

'So tell me,' Jopi said to Hannah. 'What was Neville like as a little boy?'

'Oh, hopeless!' Neville said, before Hannah could speak. 'The perfect nerd! Billy-no-mates. You wouldn't recognise me – I was weedy and skinny – not like now,' he poked his paunch regretfully, to make them laugh. 'Hannah, now – she hasn't changed at all! The moment I saw her I was transported back to primary school!'

'It's true!' said Jopi. 'You've not aged in all the time I've known you!'

'Of course, you are only twenty,' said Isabelle and everyone laughed again.

'I wonder how many friends we would recognise from

school,' said Jopi. 'Some people change so much. Me – I was always the naughty one!'

'So, no change there,' said Karl, leaning forward. Was he flirting with her? Jopi had that effect on younger men.

'I don't think we really change,' said Heidi. 'Inside, I am still ten years old!'

'Me too,' said Jopi, 'and then I look in the mirror!'

'But the child is still there,' said Neville. 'In the eyes.'

'L'enfant reste toujours dans l'esprit,' Isabelle said, smiling fondly at Hannah. As if she knew her. As if any of them did.

She put her glass down. 'But then, aren't we wasting our time?' she said, looking round at them all. 'Isn't it our business to help people to mature?'

Heidi said, 'But do we ever leave that child behind?'

'Would we want to?' Jopi said.

Hannah filled her glass again. She felt a dark, primitive urge, emboldening. 'But don't you find it irritating,' she said, 'when you meet someone from the past, who thinks you are still as you were thirty or forty years ago? That you haven't moved on?'

She was looking at Jopi, not Neville.

'True,' Karl said. 'That's what families are like. I have two older sisters and whenever I go back home, I'm always the baby of the family!' He pulled a face then beamed.

Jopi glanced from Hannah to Neville. 'Perhaps you should tell us what Hannah was like as a little girl?' she said.

Neville sat back, appraising her. Hannah raised her eyes slowly, staring back. 'Oh, she was a goody-goody,' he said. 'She never put a foot wrong. Always first in class, first to hand in her homework. Teacher's helper . . .'

Hannah felt a spark of rage.

'So, you were a good little girl?' asked Jopi.

worked hard,' Hannah said. 'I realised, early on, that I
...d get nothing without working for it.'

'And so quiet!' Neville said. 'You would hardly know she
was there.'

You knew, Hannah thought. She could feel her neck flush-
ing from the wine.

'That *is* how women get on,' said Heidi. 'Being the rebel,
the loud one, only works for boys!'

'And she did get on,' Neville said to Heidi. 'Look at her
now!'

'Things change,' Hannah said.

'Only on the surface,' said Neville. 'I'm sure you still work
hard at being good. At what you do,' he added.

Hannah felt her face flush as well as her neck. 'You see
that's what I mean,' she said, looking at Heidi, then Jopi. 'That
kind of thinking – it's another kind of stereotyping. It's lazy.'

She looked at Neville then and saw something flare in
his eyes. 'And, in certain respects, cruel,' she went on. 'Isn't
that what we try to avoid? Pigeon-holing people – especially
children – marking them out as naughty or deviant or good,
so they carry that label with them for the rest of their lives?'

'Well,' said Neville, smiling at her, 'why don't you tell us
what you were really like?'

'Oh, not on the first night!' cried Jopi. 'We should save that
for the final evening!'

Everyone laughed, and the talk turned to the itinerary for
the rest of the conference. Isabelle said she'd thought they
would eat out on the following evening – she'd planned a little
tour, and on the last night a river cruise and a meal on the
boat. This was greeted with delight by Karl, Heidi and Neville.

'There will be others joining us,' Isabelle said. 'Lots of
people here have never been to Geneva before, and it's so

beautiful, it would be a pity to leave without seeing it properly.'

'Of course, Hannah knows it very well,' Jopi said. 'So if you like, we could do something different?'

But Hannah said she had her own plans. 'Do go with the others,' she said to Jopi.

'You're sure?'

'I've got lots to do. And I still have to work on my lecture.'

'Well, but we will see you at some of the sessions?' Jopi said. 'Heidi is speaking tomorrow, and Neville on the following day.'

Neville was looking at her with that cynical smile, eyebrow raised. 'Of course,' she said. What else could she say? 'I wouldn't miss it.' She looked away from him.

'Good, then – that's all settled,' Jopi said.

The conversation moved on to who had visited Switzerland before, and when and where, while all around them currents of noise from the neighbouring tables rose and fell, and through the great glass wall the lake lay like a pale shadow, paler now than the sky.

Just for a moment, but with a piercing clarity, Hannah saw that other stretch of water superimposed upon it, its greenish lights, its smooth surface, almost opaque. She blinked, once, twice, and met Neville's eyes. He smiled sadly and looked away.

There was a discussion about dessert, but Heidi said she never ate dessert any more, and she didn't want to be too late getting to bed – it was an early start for her in the morning. Hannah seized the opportunity. 'Me too,' she said, picking up her bag.

'But you don't have to get up early,' Jopi protested.

'I always do, though,' Hannah said. 'I like to walk first thing, before breakfast.'

'Which room are you in?' asked Neville, and she flinched.

'I'm sorry?' she said.

'I was hoping we might have a chance to catch up at some point.'

'I'm sure we—' Hannah began, but Karl interrupted, 'You can't just ask ladies for their room number - people will get the wrong idea!'

Karl was drunk, of course, but everyone laughed politely, and Isabelle said, 'Ladies! Whoever uses that word any more?' Jopi said she liked it and was thinking of reclaiming it, then Heidi stood up decisively, saying if she ate any more she'd have indigestion all night, and gratefully, Hannah stood up too.

'Good night,' she said. 'Sleep well.' And before the good-byes could become protracted, she began making her way between the tables, waiting for people to adjust their chairs.

Heidi followed her, saying something, but it was noisier now, so many people, all those strands of conversation rising on a tide of wine. Hannah could still hear Jopi's laugh as they left, and see the shining curve of the lake through the glass.

'That's better,' Heidi said, as soon as they were through the doors. 'I love conferences, but they're so exhausting - mainly because one has to be sociable!'

Hannah smiled.

'Ah - there you are!' Heidi said, retrieving her card key from the depths of her bag. It was a capacious bag, with an old-fashioned clasp. 'One year I lost it and it caused no end of trouble! Well - I'm only one floor up - I should take the stairs.'

'The lift for me,' Hannah said. Heidi closed the clasp of her bag. 'I'll see you tomorrow then. Be careful of that Neville chap,' she added. 'I think he has eyes for you!' She smiled her sharp smile and walked away before Hannah could reply.

V

IN THE LIFT, Hannah stood pressed between two men in suits, a woman with an orange perm and a young man in overalls who looked as though he might work in the kitchen. Forced into such intimate proximity, no one spoke. On the fourth floor Hannah got out and glanced quickly both ways along the corridor as though Neville might have followed her after all. Relieved, she let herself into her room.

She prised the sandals off her feet and took out her phone. There was a message from Thibaut – he'd called her while she was in the restaurant but she'd been too distracted by Neville's arrival to answer. Thibaut said he was sorry he'd missed her earlier, he'd gone to dinner with the new lecturer and the visiting professor. He was tired now, and was probably going to get an early night. Perhaps they could speak in the morning.

I miss you, he said.

If only she'd taken the call!

But what could she have said at the table, with everyone there? *Come and get me now?*

It was too late to phone him; Thibaut needed his sleep. She worried about him and his work ethic, his refusal to accept the demands of aging.

Besides, what would Neville think if she left the conference? Would he come looking for her?

What did he *want*?

She studied the programme again. Today was Thursday,

Neville would speak on Saturday. Hannah would give the keynote speech at the end of the conference, on Sunday. There was a lecture before hers, by someone called Anton Lavigne, who was a newcomer, an early-career researcher. It was about the effects of opto-genetic stimulation in the treatment of dementia. Thibaut would have been interested in that.

Neville's slot was at the same time as another lecture, given by Dr Maryam Abimbola, from Nigeria. Hannah would have liked to have gone to that. She'd watched a TED talk Dr Abimbola had given once, about mental health problems in Nigeria, and the uses and abuses of traditional medicines.

Surely she didn't have to go to Neville's lecture? She should avoid him as much as possible. It was only three days. After her lecture on Sunday there would be a lunch for all the delegates, and then she could go home. To Thibaut.

Carefully, Hannah lay down on the bed, resting her cheek on her hand the way she used to do when she was small. Her eyelids closed, the confusion of thoughts gradually settling like sediment, floating down.

The reservoir was a large pool at the bottom of a slope that was overhung with trees. In their shade, the water was a sullen green. There were clusters of reeds, blonde stalks standing up from it, and to one side, a collection of lily pads, flat, and broad.

There was the stone bridge with the rusted railing, there the little platform, jutting into the water. Large pebbles stippled the banks. They were slippery with moss.

Joanna had said they weren't slippery.

'Jump!' Joanna's voice cried, and Hannah's eyes flew open, staring into the dark.

There was a pounding sensation in her chest and her

stomach: her heart, and the vagus nerve, clamouring for attention. Something was moving outside her door.

Footsteps came nearer, retreated again.

Then returned.

The crease of light beneath the door was snuffed out suddenly. Hannah lay rigid on the bed.

She should phone reception. But what would she say? There's someone outside my room, in the corridor?

It was probably someone who'd had too much to drink, and gone to the wrong door.

In a sudden, fierce movement, Hannah swung her legs off the bed. At the same time something was pushed beneath the door. She heard a man's voice, a muffled curse. The footsteps retreated again.

Swiftly, almost silently, Hannah hurried to the door. She pressed her fingertips to it for a moment, but the sound of footsteps had disappeared. She waited for one second, two, then switched on the light.

There was a scrap of paper on the carpet. Even before she picked it up, Hannah knew who it was from.

Dear Hannah, it's so good to see you again. I'm sorry there was no chance to talk. You were kind enough to say you would attend my lecture, the day after tomorrow. Perhaps you'd like to have lunch afterwards in the little bistro? There's a roof garden, and a veggie menu. It would be great to catch up. N.

Hannah straightened slowly, gripping the note so tightly her fingertips went numb. Then, in another quick movement she opened the door, looking along the corridor to the left and right.

Nothing. The corridor was vibrant with electric lighting, but empty. A long line of anonymous doors, the lift.

She hadn't heard the lift. Was it possible they were on the same floor? Or had he taken the stairs?

How had he known the room number?

Jopi, or Isabelle, must have given it to him. She could imagine him asking, casually, as though entitled, and they wouldn't have seen a reason to refuse. He wanted to see his old friend.

Hannah closed the door again, leaned against it for a moment, then looked back at the note.

It would be great to catch up. N.

What should she do?

She wasn't going to meet him, that was certain. But she could hardly claim she hadn't seen the note.

That was why he'd pushed it through her door.

Hannah returned to her bed and sat on the edge of it. She considered crumpling the paper, dropping it into the bin that would be emptied by the cleaners, then she looked at it again.

Perhaps you'd like to have lunch afterwards . . .

She could feel the corners of her mouth pulling down. Thibaut would tease her about it. *Always so worried,* he would say.

Perhaps she should go to meet Neville. Would he give up otherwise? He could find her work email easily enough, she imagined him finding her address, intruding himself into her life here in Switzerland, with Thibaut.

Unthinkable.

He would know how far he could go without actually stalking her. How much distress he could cause.

She felt mildly ill, as though worms were squirming in her stomach. But it was ridiculous, she was a professional woman, where was her training now?

What was the worst he could do?

Despite her anxiety, Hannah yawned suddenly, hugely. The digital clock on the computer told her it was 2.26 – and she wasn't even undressed yet. She'd fallen asleep in her clothes! What was the matter with her? She could almost feel herself unravelling, layer by layer. She had tried so hard, for so many years, and this was all it took.

She shouldn't take any decision now, at this time of night. The early hours were the very worst time for rational thought.

Overcoming a certain resistance, Hannah undressed, hanging up her clothes or folding them neatly, methodically. She couldn't escape the feeling of being watched.

She needed to sleep, or she wouldn't wake up in time for the conference. Which would be one kind of solution, she supposed.

But she couldn't keep trying to avoid Neville, that much was obvious. He was determined to see her.

Hannah sat down again on the edge of her bed. She felt another powerful impulse to call Thibaut. But if she rang now, at this time, it would frighten him, he would think it was an emergency. She couldn't do that to him.

But she wanted her husband. She needed him to anchor her to their world.

VI

THE STREET WHERE Hannah used to live was bounded at both ends by larger roads, and lined with trees, which her mother seemed to think gave it an aura of respectability or distinction. Otherwise, there was nothing to distinguish it from any other street. It was not especially long, nor short, elegant or squalid. Only a closer examination revealed its more interesting aspects.

At the bottom end, where Hannah and her mother lived, there were terraced houses. Two-up-two down, straight-on-to-the-pavement houses, with no gardens, but at the back, a small, paved yard. These yards had, at one time contained an outside toilet, but along with most other people on the street, Hannah's mum had installed a bathroom inside. This meant that Hannah's bedroom, always small, became a box room, not much larger than a cupboard, while the outside toilet became a shed.

Part-way up the hill were the semis, where Joanna lived. These had bay windows and gardens. A small garden to the front of each house, and a larger one behind, with lawns and privets.

Each of these semis had three bedrooms and three rooms downstairs. Although, in Joanna's house at least, the kitchen was tiny, smaller than Hannah's, and Joanna's bedroom was also small, like Hannah's. Joanna's two older brothers occupied a larger room, and their parents what was called, rather grandly, the master bedroom.

Beyond the semis, at the top of the street, there was a wall, and behind this wall were the mysterious, detached residences of the fairly rich. Mysterious in that no one ever saw the residents. They didn't go to the corner shop, or stand gossiping on the street. Their children did not play out but were ferried to ballet classes, horse riding, or chess.

The other side of the street was a replica of Hannah's side, except at the top end, where, instead of detached residences, there was a sports field belonging to the local college.

This street where Hannah lived, at number 26, formed the backdrop to her childhood. She didn't see it as a microcosm of the class system in England until much later. Or as culpable, in any way, for what happened there. Only after she'd moved away from it, taken her degree and several professional qualifications, did it acquire this extra significance in her mind. She saw clearly, then, how rigidly the social distinctions were enforced. The different groups kept to themselves. The children from the terraces did not play with the children from the semis, the children from the detached houses didn't play at all.

Only the trees linked them all, stately sycamores with scarred trunks, shedding their bark in summer, winged seeds and leaves in autumn, when the pavements were spattered with yellow, russet and red. The leaves were moist, untidy, beautiful. People slipped on them and complained.

Over the years that Hannah lived on the street, there were many changes. People were born or died, children grew up, families came and went, households split. There were attic conversions, kitchen extensions, outside toilets became sheds. Double glazing was installed, front gardens were paved over to accommodate cars, roofs were stripped and renewed. The road was dug up by the gas board, then by varying power companies, then because of the drains. Potholes were mended, streetlamps replaced, BT vans and tree surgeons came and went. At the top end the pavement was widened because of the college students, at the bottom end the shop closed because of the supermarket (which was cheaper, but further away). There were arguments about parking, or extensions, and noise. One man painted the brick walls of his house a lurid red, with the words EVERYTHING THEY TELL YOU IS A LIE sprawling across the front. The people who moved in after him spent some time removing it.

Only the Rules didn't change, even when Asian families moved in. The wealthy Asian family, with two children in a large, detached house, had nothing to do with the more populous family that moved into the terraced house opposite Hannah. The rules were unspoken, and therefore sacrosanct. They were only broken by Hannah and Joanna.

Usually, Joanna played with Alison, and sometimes Susan, who was more than a year younger, but also from the semis. They played in their bedrooms or gardens. Hannah didn't play with them, and she wasn't allowed to play with the other children from the terraces. Her mother didn't want her to play with *rough children*, which included all the children who played out on the street, rather than in the gardens.

There weren't many children, in any case, that Hannah might have played with. The terraces contained a number of older people whose families had moved away. Next door there were two teenage boys, and next to them, an elderly couple, then a family with three little boys who were definitely *rough*. They spat in the street and kicked balls against neighbouring doors, screamed *Paki* after various members of the Asian family, whom Hannah's mother referred to as *coloured*.

Hannah's mother hardly thought it necessary to stipulate that Hannah shouldn't play with them; in any case, boys didn't play with girls. The Asian family kept to themselves. Wendy and Aileen also lived on the other side of the street, but they played together, skipping or two-ball, against the short wall at the end of the houses. Sometimes their mothers stood out, talking in the street. Wendy's mother had a laugh like a scream. Rough.

Hannah's mother never stood gossiping in the street. She sent Hannah to the shop rather than going herself. She acted almost like one of the mothers from the detached houses, 'giving herself airs', for no reason anyone could think of, a woman without a husband, who worked as a cleaner in the local hospital.

She was also, as Hannah gradually came to see, definitely odd. Summer or winter she wore a brown overcoat like a man's, her hair starched into a stiff perm, a mauve hat on top of it that had the shape and whorled texture of a brain. Each day she walked up the sloping street to work, a severe, slightly off-kilter woman, whose horizons had narrowed, who had developed a certain rigidity that manifested itself in her walk and in her domestic habits. A purblind quality: this must go here, that there. The randomness inherent in the universe was not to be acknowledged, or if it was acknowledged, contended with. Dust and grime, litter, smears on the window that were revealed mercilessly whenever the sun shone, the tendency of small objects to go astray – these things were her natural enemies and she fought them with a vengeful rage. On the street people drew away from her, almost imperceptibly, as she passed. No one came to play at Hannah's house.

The last thing Hannah's mother would say to her, before she set off to work, was that she was to stay in, and be good.

But soon as her mother left, Hannah would lift the rusty latch on the back yard gate, struggling a little, afraid, each time that it wouldn't give, experiencing a thrill of joy when it did, then make her way along one tiny, uneven alleyway after another, picking her way through the debris and the stones, into the Wild.

Which was where she'd met Joanna.

VII

HANNAH WOKE, BLURRED and heavy as if con-
densed by sleep. The digital clock informed her it was
6:42. She'd slept for perhaps three hours. Today was the first
day of the conference.

She felt numb. Even the pang of dread she experienced, as
she remembered what had woken her last night, seemed dull,
like the echo of a stone dropped into a well.

Dense cloud had descended overnight. Through the
window the vast lake gave off a spectral light. There was
something hypnotic about it. Hannah lay for a while, gazing
at the pale expanse.

Slowly it altered, ghostly shapes becoming visible, seams
of white on the far mountains.

Despite visiting Geneva regularly, Hannah didn't know
the names of the different peaks. In any case, in this light the
different shapes merged, unemphatic like the pale watercolours
of a Japanese painting. A dark ribbon of birds twisted across
the unobtrusive seam between sky and water, configuring and
reconfiguring.

Hannah remained where she was, as though she could fend
off the day, although already it was gathering force in her
mind.

If she wanted to phone Thibaut, she should do it soon,
before he set off for the University. And yet, somehow, in
the night, as confused dreams had shifted in kaleidoscopic

revolutions, she'd come to a decision about that. She wasn't going to ask her husband to come and collect her. She wasn't going to run away, or act as though she'd done something wrong. She wasn't even going to stay in her room.

In a moment she would shower and dress, and go to the cafe for breakfast, although she was still not hungry after last night's meal. And then she would make her way to the lecture theatre, to hear the first lecture of the day.

'Too much to drink,' said Heidi, shaking pills from a little box. 'I should never drink wine so late.'

'Have more water,' said Hannah, pouring into her glass.

'Water upsets my digestion,' Heidi said. She wore a different woollen outfit today, purple embroidered with red. Her face was crumpled, baffled by the complexities of light and noise and food.

'Of course, I would be giving the lecture,' she grumbled.

'You'll be fine,' Hannah said, bracingly.

Heidi swallowed a tablet with her orange juice. 'No one will come anyway,' she said. 'And even if they do, they won't listen.'

'I'll be there,' Hannah encouraged her. 'I'll listen.'

Heidi pulled a face. 'No pressure then – you – the keynote speaker!'

Evidently, she would not be comforted. Hannah started to change the subject, but Heidi said, 'There's your friend,' and her stomach gave one of those little contractions, as though it were a heart.

For there, indeed, he was, talking animatedly with a younger man, not Karl, and piling pastries onto his plate.

What had she expected? She'd come to the cafe even though she knew she might see him.

34

Heidi was looking at her quizzically. 'It is uncomfortable, no? When someone turns up from your past.'

Hannah shook her head a little, glancing down at her plate. 'It's fine,' she said.

'It's not fine,' said Heidi. 'I noticed that last night.'

Really? Hannah always prided herself on giving nothing away. Was it just that she'd had too much to drink?

Heidi was looking at her narrowly. 'I'm sorry,' she said, 'Ignore me. Blame it on nerves.'

Obviously, Hannah was actually transparent, to Heidi at least. 'No, it's fine,' she repeated. 'It's just – I didn't know him that well – but he's acting as though we're long-lost friends . . .'

'Disconcerting,' Heidi said. 'Sometimes we have such an impact on other people – so much more than we think, or intend.'

'Mmm,' Hannah said vaguely, discouragingly. She was watching Neville. Had he seen them? Would he come over to join them?

But no, he appeared to be leaving with the younger man, carrying coffee and pastries. Even as she allowed herself a small wash of relief she wondered, *Where is he going?*

'—and then they shatter us,' Heidi said.

'I'm sorry?'

'These people,' Heidi said. 'They keep you in a kind of mould in their minds, and when they return, whether they know it or not, it's to shatter that mould. But the danger is, that in the process, they shatter us.'

Hannah opened her mouth to say something, then changed her mind.

'Or set us free,' Heidi went on. 'But you know, in all my years of practice, I've discovered freedom is the last thing people want. What they tell you is, *I'm not the person I used to be*. But what they mean is, *I will never, under any circumstances, let that person go*. That's what I should have called my paper,' she said, frowning at the copy of the programme that lay between them. '*Never let me go* – you know – like the novel? Or the film.' Hannah hadn't even noticed the title of Heidi's talk, but she saw it now. *Redactions of Culpability in the Judicial Process*.

'Too late now,' muttered Heidi, closing the clasp on her bag. It popped open again because of the pressure of paper. Heidi sighed.

Hannah carried one of Heidi's bulging files down some steps on the far side of the atrium to a door. As they entered the lecture theatre its space seemed to amplify around them. Hannah put the file down on the lectern in front of the screen, without looking up. 'There you are,' she said to Heidi. 'Do you need anything else?'

Heidi was burrowing in her immense bag. 'Here it is!' She held up her memory stick triumphantly. 'Now,' she said. 'To work out where to put it . . .'

She glanced towards the control panel, which was extensive.

'I'm sure there'll be someone to help,' Hannah said.

'Yes, yes – we're early,' Heidi said, turning towards the lectern.

Hannah stepped back, then for the first time, glanced around the theatre.

It was empty. She felt a wash of relief. She turned back to Heidi, making conventional noises of reassurance and encouragement. Did she want her to call Jopi? Or Isabelle?

'No, no,' Heidi said, waving an arm. 'Please – sit.'

Hannah made her way up the wide steps towards the back of the theatre and sat at the end of a row. Only after she'd pushed her bag beneath her seat did she look up again.

Still empty. Perhaps Heidi had been right about no one attending. Although hadn't Neville said he would come?

Just as she was thinking this, the door to one side of the theatre opened. Hannah's heart leapt. But it was only the student volunteer, Pierre. He fussed around Heidi, helping her to switch on the screen, test the sound, set up the first slide.

Then a different door opened and Isabelle entered carrying bottles of water. She was wearing a short grey shirt dress, almost entirely without shape, and studded ankle boots. She spoke rapidly to Pierre, gesturing towards the air-conditioning, the overhead projector, and then to Heidi as Pierre disappeared.

Gradually, the first people filtered in. They arranged themselves in groups along the rows, one or two of them sitting alone. Hannah dipped her head as they arrived, consciously studying the programme.

A man made his way up the steps towards Hannah's row. He wore horn-rimmed glasses and an expression of bleak fury. Hannah prepared to move, but he stopped at the row below Hannah's and sat immediately in front of her. Annoyed, Hannah shifted slightly. Why did people do that when they had a whole row of seats to choose from? But it was all right, she could still see. The lecture theatre was very well designed.

More people arrived. A group of women made their way along Hannah's row from the other end. Hannah concentrated on the programme. Heidi would speak until 10.45, then there would be a break, and then another speaker, Klara Ebber at 11.00.

Then lunch.

Perhaps you'd like to have lunch afterwards, Neville's note had said. But that was tomorrow, not today. Today she would try to avoid having lunch with anyone. And tomorrow? She would put him off somehow. Hannah looked at the clock. It was already time for the lecture to begin, but people were still arriving. Just like students. Universities had long ago given up their policy of not admitting latecomers to a lecture.

She glanced around the theatre again, and this time she saw Neville, entering through the side door. He was with the same young man she'd seen in the cafe. He made his way over to Heidi and spoke to her briefly. She nodded, distracted, with a frowning smile.

From her vantage point Hannah took in everything about him; the grey T-shirt, with UNIVERSITY OF AUCKLAND printed across it in navy, a circular logo stretched over his stomach, a dark jacket that was probably once black, now faded, crumpled chinos and trainers. He carried a canvas bag, slung over one shoulder. THE CAKE FACTORY was printed across it.

It was almost compulsory for male academics to dress like elderly students. 'See how chilled I am,' they seemed to be saying. 'I'm one of you.' From above, Hannah could see how his hair was thinning, there was a pinkish, freckled crown surrounded by a straggly halo of ginger-grey curls.

She was surprised by the intensity of her attention, the strength of her loathing.

Neville finished talking to Heidi and made his way over to where his friend was sitting, two rows from the front. Typically, he made everyone on the row move. The acoustics were such that his apologies travelled around the theatre, *Oh, I'm so sorry, I'm so clumsy, do you mind? That's really kind of you.*

She watched him take a sheaf of paper out of his bag, drop it, and disturb everyone again as he picked it up.

But at least he didn't look round.

Heidi tapped the microphone and coughed into it lightly, then reached for her bag. Hannah closed her eyes, pressed one finger between her eyebrows and rubbed it slowly towards her hairline. Acupressure.

When she opened her eyes, Neville was looking directly at her.

There was that leap of terror, inexplicable, unjustifiable. She thought he might wave at her to come down and sit with him, or worse, leave his seat to sit with her, but he simply stared at her, unsmiling.

They remained that way for a long moment, her gaze locked with his.

Then he nodded, slowly, once, and turned back towards the front.

Hannah was actually gripping the arms of her chair. Her mouth was dry. When she released her fingers she realised they were trembling. She should leave, she thought. She could still leave. But just at that moment, Heidi spoke.

'Is this all right?' she said. 'Can everyone hear me?'

There was a murmur of assent. Hannah clasped her hands together and gazed only at Heidi. *You can do this*, she told herself.

The headline, *Redactions of Culpability*, appeared on the screen.

There was some coughing and further shuffling as more people arrived, then Heidi began.

She gave an overview of the age of criminal responsibility, which varied so much from one country to another. It was 13 in France, 14 in Italy, and Germany, 16 in Cuba, Argentina, the Russian Federation and Hong Kong. In the UK, as in Switzerland, it was ten. Although Scotland differed from

England and Wales, having changed its ACR to 12 some years ago.

Hannah glanced down at Neville's naked, speckled crown, then towards the nearest exit. Maybe she could leave early, before the end.

'UK law used to include the principle of *doli incapax*, which stated that a child under 14 is not capable of criminal intent. In practical terms this meant it was up to the prosecution to prove the child fully knew what they were doing . . .'

You knew what you were doing, Hannah's mother said.

Hannah's mother was dead, of course, and couldn't very well have said anything. Extraordinary how the mind could snag itself on some memory, trip you up.

'—abolished in 1998. Why? Because of evidence-based research? No. The UK government decided we should all "stop making excuses for children who offend".'

None of this was news. There had been years of debate about the ACR in the UK throughout Europe. No one agreed with it; the movement to raise it was hardly even controversial. Except that it was still there, unchanged.

Hannah supposed Heidi was laying out her stall, preparing for some startling revelation or proposition. That, after all, was the point of this conference. It wasn't the usual academic symposium; it was for those people who thought, as Jopi put it, *hors du cadre*, outside the frame.

Nothing Heidi had said so far was *outside the frame*.

'—current research into brain function tells us there are many challenges caused by immaturity. Adolescence, for instance, represents a phase of increased impulsivity and sensation-seeking as well as a heightened vulnerability to peer influence, which all have an impact upon decision-making.'

Hannah looked back down towards Neville. He was leaning

forward, apparently absorbed by what Heidi was sayir

If Hannah left the lecture early, to avoid seeing him, she would still have to find a way to tell him she didn't want to meet him for lunch. She couldn't simply ignore the note, she would have to respond.

She could tell him she was visiting a friend in Geneva. Or two friends, one on each day of the conference.

Perhaps Heidi could pass the message on.

Of course, Heidi might ask her what she'd thought about the lecture. With an effort Hannah returned her attention to it.

'—capacity for abstract reasoning matures throughout adolescence. It is significantly underdeveloped in children aged 11 to 13 years. It is still developing at 14 to 15 years, and even at 16 to 17,' Heidi said. 'And, of course, children in the criminal justice system are more likely to suffer from learning difficulties than those who are not.'

She should take notes, perhaps, so that she could refer to Heidi's lecture in her own. Hannah reached beneath her seat for her bag. She would normally use her phone for notes, but didn't want to switch it on here, in the lecture theatre.

'—important work of researchers such as Professor Rossier,' Heidi said.

Everyone turned towards Hannah. She felt a foolish impulse to hide. She straightened slowly. *Don't look! Don't look!* she cried silently.

Neville wasn't looking. Or if he had looked briefly, he had turned back towards the front.

'I'm sure Professor Rossier will explain it to you in far more detail than I can. We are all very much looking forward to hearing more about the scientific data in your lecture,' Heidi said, warmly. Hannah managed to nod and smile.

What was the matter with her? Why was she reacting like a child? It was as though layers of adulthood had been peeled away from her. Or a shell had cracked exposing the damp chick, fragile, incapable.

A diagram had appeared on the screen, a rudimentary map of the different areas of the brain. The attention of the room turned back towards it. Slowly, Hannah's tension began to subside.

'At any rate, it's now understood that adolescence is a period of significant neurodevelopment,' Heidi continued. 'Maturation may not conclude until the mid-twenties, in fact, with the full development of the prefrontal cortex.

'This means that the child in prison, unlike the adult, will undergo dramatic changes as they mature. This should have implications for the possibility of rehabilitation for them, for *leaving the past behind.*'

Hannah had changed almost everything about herself since childhood, her name, her nationality, her language, her accent, her class. All the cells of her body, according to physical science, had also changed.

Anyone would think she might have left the past behind.

Hannah glanced at Neville again. Evidently, he hadn't left the past behind, either. Or why was he here?

'Children who are categorised as offenders are more likely to perceive themselves as criminals, engage in criminal behaviour and associate with criminal peers. They are more likely to be sexually assaulted in prison than in juvenile facilities, or co-opted into further crime. On release, they have to disclose criminal records when they apply for educational courses or employment, so in many cases, they are less likely to enter or complete their education, which, in turn, reduces the possibility of employment.

'Is it enough, therefore, to campaign for the reintroduction of *doli incapax?*'

Hannah was reminded suddenly and powerfully of one of her first cases. A young boy called Michael.

Hannah had met Michael when he was 11 years old. He was pleasant, helpful, with the kind of blond good looks regularly found on old knitting patterns or in Ladybird books about Janet and John, where John helps his father in the garage, or pushes his younger sister on a swing.

In this case, Michael had pounded his younger sister to death with a brick and pissed on her as she died.

'She wouldn't shut up,' he'd said.

Asked when he'd first had the urge to kill his sister, he'd said, 'I always wanted to.'

He'd been ten years old at the time of the attack, and his sister, seven. An excellent defence lawyer had seen to it that the principle of *doli incapax* had been applied to his case, which was why he hadn't been imprisoned but put in care. Teams of people, including Hannah, had devoted themselves to him, in the hope of justifying the retention of *doli incapax*, which was already under threat. They'd hoped to shed light on his motivations, also, perhaps, to find a different Michael concealed within him, tender, bruised, innocent of evil intent. They wrote extensive case notes and made regretful diagnoses of *empathy deficiency* or, more hopefully, *delay*.

Michael wasn't difficult like some of the other children; he was considerate, socially aware. *Well brought up.* None of the usual profiles fitted. His parents, while not well-off, could be classed as lower middle class, his mother a primary school teacher, his father a surveyor. They seemed loving, they went to church.

His mother didn't visit Michael all the time he was in care, but his father did. Hannah could remember his face, earnest, eroded. He would sit with his son in the visiting room, not saying much, sometimes holding his hand.

Apart from his expression he looked very much like his son, as if they might both have modelled knitwear, or stepped from the pages of a Ladybird book.

As Hannah's sessions with Michael continued, she began to feel a kind of bond between them. He preferred seeing her, she was sure, to the other therapists. There was no reason for this, nothing expressed, nothing tangible, just a subtle alteration of energy when he entered the room and realised she was there.

Then one day the vicar of the local church had visited. He'd spoken to all the children about the God of love, not judgement, and how He was present everywhere, in nature, and in themselves.

Afterwards, they had taken the children to a country park. There was a lake full of birds, diving, floating, skimming above the water, and Kevin, one of the assistants, had taken pains to teach them all the different names. Then, just as he was pointing to a duckling swimming furiously behind its mother, a heron had swooped down and swallowed it in a single gulp. You could see the shape of it travelling down its neck.

There were cries of disgust and delight, gagging noises. Michael had turned to Hannah. His normally bland expression had shifted into something else. 'God got hungry,' he said.

He was articulate, Michael, witty, even. Perhaps she had suppressed a smile.

'Tint *God*,' one of the other boys, Danny Millfield, had said. 'S'instinct.'

Michael shrugged. 'Where's that come from then?'

Danny said, 'From *them*, not *God!*'

Michael raised his eyebrows, spread his hands. 'Where'd *they* come from?'

Danny, challenged, reacted in his usual way, with aggression. 'You think you're so clever, shithead—'

'That's enough, Danny,' Kevin said.

'Well, tell him then,' Danny said. 'Tint God – he dunt get hungry!'

'How would you know?' asked Michael.

'I think,' Hannah said, 'Michael is just pointing out that it doesn't make sense to attribute everything to God.' *Or we'd need a very different idea of God*, she didn't say.

But Danny, alive with religious fervour (who knew?) had stoutly defended the deity.

'Just because God's good,' he'd said, 'dunt mean bad things can't happen.'

'I think we're on tricky ground now,' Kevin said, anxious to appease Danny, who didn't suffer from fits, but did very good imitations of them when enraged, falling to the floor, banging his head and biting. 'People have debated that one for years without getting anywhere.'

'It's not about good or bad,' Michael said. 'It's *kill* or *be killed*.' Then he had turned to Hannah. '*You'd* know that, Miss, wouldn't you?'

There was nothing in it, of course, yet the look he gave her pierced her like a dart. For an instant she'd actually felt cold.

She could have challenged him, asked him what he meant. But she'd seen his response to all the weighted, angled questions asked by police and social workers, therapists like herself:

Why do you say that?

What do you mean by that, Michael?

She'd watched the shutters of his face coming down.

In any case, he was already walking away. So she'd

murmured something about the survival instinct, attempting to mollify Danny, then changed the subject to distract him.

Probably, she'd reasoned with herself, Michael had seen a look of scepticism on her face as the vicar had spoken.

That was all.

But it wasn't the only time he'd made pointed remarks, obliquely, with insinuations that were hardly worth challenging, always unsettling.

What did he see in her?

What could he know?

Nothing, of course. Nobody knew.

It was one of those tricks of memory that brought him back so palpably now, distracting her. Hannah's mind had wandered completely away from the lecture. Reluctantly, she pulled it back.

'—brought up in care, or in violent, extremely poor households where health and safety were luxuries their families could not afford. They may already have been physically or sexually abused when very young.'

None of this was true of Michael.

'The fact is that punishment in such cases will not prevent re-offending. And then, of course, they are punished again, more severely, and their behaviour worsens and so the cycle repeats. The fact that one in three children reoffends within a year of release speaks for itself,' Heidi said.

Had Michael re-offended? It was possible, likely, even, if someone got in his way. Like his sister. Otherwise, Hannah could imagine him doing very well in the world, in politics, say, or finance. Not like Danny Millfield, who couldn't concentrate from one moment to the next. 'What are we doing, now?' he would ask repeatedly, plaintively, like a bird-call. 'What can I do now?'

Danny had re-offended, possibly out of sheer boredom. Driven by some internal lack, some need that he hadn't wished for – it had just been bestowed upon him, by genes, perhaps. Or some malignant god.

Then there was Martin Hawkes, thin, underdeveloped, who never sat when she tried to interview him, but stood to one side of the room, not responding to any of the objects she presented to him.

Ah, the parade of faces through her memory!

Michael would be in his thirties now. What had happened to him? Had his parents survived? What had happened to them? Had his father continued to support him?

'As we know, the costs of criminal proceedings against young people are enormous. Six million pounds are spent on court appearances alone.'

A list of costs appeared on screen. Heidi analysed them, the ways in which they were misleading, the *redactions of culpability* they represented.

'So, we can see that the youth justice system as it stands is both immensely expensive and ineffective. And there are alternatives. There is, for instance, the treatment pioneered in Wisconsin.'

She outlined the programme, which combined the methods of a traditional correctional institution with the therapeutic treatments of a private psychiatric facility. Then she leaned over the lectern. A sheet of paper fell to the floor.

'Alternatively,' she said, ignoring it, 'it is possible that most offences committed by children can be dealt with *in the community*. Even in the most serious cases, evidence suggests that children who are not treated as criminals, who are reintegrated into local schools, encouraged to discuss their behaviour with care workers, teachers, and parents, are much more likely to be successfully rehabilitated. In such cases, there are *no* instances of re-offending behaviour.'

She stared around the theatre, as if daring anyone to challenge her.

At university, Hannah had done some research into an Inuit community, where a young man who had killed his girlfriend had been accepted back into his social group, allowed to live with his family, given productive work. But increasingly he had chosen to spend more time on his own, taking long walks away from the settlement, and one day he had not returned at all. He had walked into the snow.

Whenever she remembered that story, she could see an image of him, bowed, trudging, intermittently running. Swirls of snow rising, rapidly obscuring him from view.

It was as real to her, this image, as one of her own memories, returning to her now, in the lecture theatre, as if she had wandered into a different scene in some labyrinthine play.

'—we know crime doesn't occur simply because of the immorality of the perpetrators, but for a complex network of reasons that we as a society need to address. When a child commits a crime, we need to acknowledge that it is the failure of the society that has nurtured that child.'

Suddenly, vividly, Hannah could see the street where she'd grown up. She could smell the tarmac, the boiled mince, the washing.

'Rather than criminalising children, we should be looking at the causes of their behaviour, in order to prevent re-offending and escalations of offence. It is up to psychologists and therapists such as ourselves to implement more effective therapies for dealing with criminal behaviour in young people, to teach them to accept responsibility for what they have done—'

Neville leaned forward at this point as though he might

speak. Hannah's stomach throbbed, but he didn't move, raise his hand.

'But before that, before anything else, we need to investigate how we, as a society, accept responsibility for crime.'

Heidi took her glasses off. Without them, her eyes almost disappeared.

'This paper,' she said, 'suggests that we should abolish the criminalisation of children and young people altogether. It proposes that no one under 30 should receive a criminal record at *all*.'

A murmur rippled around the room. This was the controversial heart of Heidi's lecture. She replaced her spectacles.

'Thank you,' she said, raising her voice as the murmur increased. 'Any questions?'

'Yes?' she said to someone Hannah couldn't see.

And the questions began.

Was Dr Kruse aware that almost all crimes were committed by people under 30?

Was she implying that young people did not know the difference between right and wrong? What about child abuse? Was there not ample evidence to suggest that the child knew it was being abused? That what was happening was wrong?

There was a chorus of protest at this. Heidi had to raise her voice, then rap on the lectern like a judge. 'That is not the same thing at *all*,' she said. It had been amply demonstrated that even tiny children knew when they were being abused. To know that one was abused, that what was happening to *oneself* was wrong, did not require the same moral development as deciding whether to participate in criminal actions against others.

Murmurs of assent and disagreement.

'Moral development,' she said, 'is a gradual thing. It's not like learning to walk, where one day the child can't, and the next day, *pouf!* – it is running into the furniture! It has been definitively proved that the relevant parts of the brain might take more than 25 years to fully develop. Which is why I'm suggesting that we do not punish anyone under 30.'

Hannah sat back as the arguments continued. She felt a complex flux of emotions: a hollow sensation, vindication, something like envy. It was all too late for her.

Soon after *the incident* Hannah's mother had bought a lock for her bedroom door, to keep her safe, she said, while she was at work. Hannah knew it was to keep her away from the Wild. It said a lot about her state of mind that she didn't even argue. She had no desire to go into the Wild again; she thought of it fearfully, as a threat. So she'd stayed in her room until her mother returned, supplied with food and a drink. She kept the curtains drawn, because she couldn't shake the sense of being watched. Unseen, the street had its own rough music, a thrum and shudder, punctuated by cries or voices, the vibrations of ordinary life in which she was no longer included.

Now, forty years later, Hannah could wonder why they had never moved, why they'd stayed on that street where the rumours continued to circulate about the odd woman with her odd child. There had been no chance of reintegration into that community. Would she have wanted it? Had she ever been part of it in the first place?

'Thank you for that,' Neville said, standing. Hannah felt a jarring uncertainty. She had completely missed what Heidi had said, what Neville was responding to. 'So, just to clarify, would you say that that even though the brain might develop empathy and remorse later in life, the process of *awareness* of the *implications* of one's own actions cannot be completed by oneself?

'Well—' Heidi began, but he interrupted her.

'In AA, for instance, it's one of the 12 steps to admit to yourself, your God *and to another person, the exact nature of your wrongs?*'

Heidi said that not everyone believed in God, of course. And there were cases where confession to another human being, purely as a relief of conscience, might do harm.

'That is surely true,' said Neville, 'if the person one confesses to has been in any way involved. But if they are neutral, objective, then surely the act of confession - or - let's use a less religious term - *acknowledgement*, is a vital part of the process for anyone?'

Neville hadn't looked in her direction even once, yet Hannah knew he was talking about her. She didn't catch what Heidi said in reply, because Neville cut across her.

'Let me put it another way,' he said, 'is it possible for the individual to rehabilitate themselves, without *publicly admitting what they have done?* Isn't rehabilitation a *participatory* process?'

Hannah could feel blood pulsing in her throat, a light sweat on her upper lip. But Heidi had had enough of being interrupted.

'We're talking about *shared responsibility*, here,' she said, a little coldly, 'but yes, of course as psychotherapists we obviously believe in the power of participation, and communication. Otherwise there would be no point to this conference, or to the profession at all.'

A small ripple of laughter ran around the theatre; it had an element of impatience in it, and derision. The other delegates had also had enough of Neville taking the floor.

'Thank you,' Neville said. 'Thank you for clarifying that.'

He sat down heavily.

Bastard! Hannah thought. But she'd known all along what he'd wanted, since the moment she'd met him in the foyer.

She felt tremulous, clammy. Someone else was asking a question, but she could hardly hear. Any moment now Neville would stand up again and point to her. *I think Professor Rossier has something to contribute to this discussion.*

She needed to leave. She looked for the clock, her glance swept past it, failing to register, then back again, *focus*. It was almost eleven. The next lecture should have started at 10.45, but Heidi was still answering questions.

Would there even be a break?

If there was, would Heidi expect Hannah to go for a coffee with her, to talk about the lecture? Would Neville decide to join them?

Hannah didn't want to go for coffee with Neville.

She reached for her bag, then, as unobtrusively as possible, manoeuvred herself out of her seat and through the nearest exit.

VIII

IN THE SHOWER room, she pressed a flannel to her face, sucking the rough texture into her mouth.

Breathe, she told herself.

She shouldn't have left. Neville might even now be relating his version of her story to all the delegates.

Breathe.

The room, with its blank tiles, seemed to be pressing in on her. She went back into the bedroom; it was no better. It was the conference centre itself that was claustrophobic, closing her in. She had to get out, she needed air.

She scrubbed her face vigorously, applied moisturiser. Then she changed into the only set of casual clothes she'd brought with her: combat trousers, a vest, canvas trainers. And a linen shirt which would serve as a jacket if the temperature cooled.

She zipped her purse and room key into her pocket and set off, walking briskly towards the exit.

As she passed the office she thought she heard Isabelle's voice shouting, *Vas te faire foutre!*

Some drama, then, but Hannah didn't want to get involved. She walked faster and the glass doors slid open for her as she left.

It was a short walk from the conference centre to the Shore Path that extended around the lake, displaying its otherworldly sheen, its inverted panoramas of mountains and trees, from one vantage point after another. As soon as Hannah reached the path, even though she wasn't wearing her regular trainers, she began to run.

Neville, she thought, as her feet pounded the path. *Neville, Neville*. What did he want from her? What did he expect her to do?

She ran past the landscaped gardens of the Public Library, swerving at one point to avoid a small dog that jumped up at her on its lead. It was a cool day with massed cloud, but people were walking through the gardens or sitting on the benches provided for viewing the lake. There was some sort of boating event going on. If anyone was surprised to see a middle-aged woman running in what were not, strictly speaking, running clothes, they didn't show it. This was Switzerland, after all, where everyone was *discret*. Everyone she passed looked down, or away.

Waves rolled like silver muscles beneath the surface of the water. Only one or two braver people were actually in it, shouting at the cold.

It had been a week or two since her last proper run and she was rapidly out of breath. She could feel a burning sensation in her lungs, a stitch coming on. She slowed down, but didn't stop. *Run through it*, that was her mantra. She'd run through foot and knee problems, against all advice, chest infections, hay fever, depression. *Run, don't stop.*

She ran through a park, then through woodland, remembering those other trees, branches whipping her arms and legs, brambles scratching. She could smell the scent of pine needles and see the imprints on her palms.

She had scrambled up the bank and slipped down again, scraping her hands and knees. Then she'd stumbled onto the path and into Neville.

Blood thrummed in Hannah's ears, her breathing was

ragged. Not good. Gradually, she slowed to a walking pace, trying to catch her breath.

He'd looked as shocked as she'd felt, she remembered that. She'd recoiled from him, she'd run away.

It was difficult to remember what had happened next: blue lights flashing, her mother's hat falling off, Joanna's mother clasping Hannah's face.

Why couldn't she remember?

Of course, she knew why she couldn't remember, she'd given papers on it. The effects of fear or threat flooded the brain with stress hormones causing the hippocampal and amygdala networks to become dissociated. With the result that few peripheral details, little or no context or time-sequence information, words or associated narrative around the stressful event could be recalled. While certain images remained highly vivid and detailed, in what was known as a flashbulb effect.

She remembered the physical sensation of bumping into Neville, the shock and fear on his face, which must have mirrored hers. But little afterwards that made sense.

Hannah was walking quite slowly now, feeling an old pain between the third and fourth toes of her left foot. She shouldn't run in these shoes – if there was one thing she'd learnt from years of running it was to wear the right shoes. What had got into her, running like a maniac in public? She must be more than a mile from the conference centre. She walked on, not limping – she wouldn't allow herself to limp – looking at the plane trees with their scaling bark, their fruit like tiny globes. The smell of them reminded her of the sycamores at home.

Home. Meaning the street where she'd grown up. Not Switzerland, where she'd lived for eleven years, married to a man she loved. Home meant the street of terraced houses where she'd lived with her mother, and the semis, where Joanna lived.

She knew, of course, because she'd been told, that she'd run to Joanna's house. No one had answered at first, she'd thought no one was in, but then Joanna's older brother, Tony, had come to the door. He'd been asleep, apparently, and she was incoherent, she couldn't get him to understand.

If she tried, she could picture Tony's face, pale, with lank brown hair, looking at her in confusion. But she didn't know if that was a real memory, or a reconstruction.

Her most vivid memory was of scrambling up that bank and bumping into Neville.

She'd recoiled from him, and he'd looked shocked. And then he'd spoken to her, those words that she'd managed to forget.

'What have you done?' he'd said.

IX

HANNAH WOVE BETWEEN tourists, someone dressed as a clown handing out leaflets, two young couples pushing trolleys.

She stopped at a patisserie, bought herself a couple of pastries, and frozen yoghurt at a kiosk. She wasn't hungry, but it meant she wouldn't have to join the others for lunch, she could stay in her room.

Was that reasonable, to stay in her room?

She couldn't bear to see Neville again.

Surely the act of confession – or – let's use a less religious term – acknowledgement, is a vital part of the process for anyone?

How dare he?

She could smell the earth of the bank, the acrid smell of the leaves.

What have you done? he'd said. Not, *what's the matter?* Or, *Are you all right?* But, *What have you done?*

She couldn't remember answering him, she could only remember running away.

What had he seen?

She'd never asked him, never had chance, really. After weeks of questioning, they'd gone, at the end of summer, to their separate schools. Their paths hadn't crossed again for forty years.

She hadn't heard, at any time during that summer, that he'd

actually accused her of anything. So why had he said those words, *What have you done?*

Hannah blinked in surprise as she registered the glass dome of the conference centre. She couldn't have described the route she'd taken, nor any of the sights she'd seen along the way.

Her memory was full of gaps, or holes, like a string vest.

There was a gap between running away from Neville and being questioned by a policewoman at her home. Her mother standing – no, sitting – but rigid as a pole at her side. And another gap, until Joanna's mother was clasping her face. She didn't want to fill them in.

Hannah felt a sudden strong aversion, almost a nausea, at the thought of going back into the conference centre.

But where else would she go? She was booked in, all her things were in her room.

She would go straight to her room and massage her foot. With any luck, she wouldn't see anyone she knew.

But as soon as she entered she could see Jopi, Heidi, Karl, gathered around Isabelle. And one of the student helpers, a young girl called Marta, with scraped-back, yellow-blonde hair.

Not Neville. With a rush of relief she saw that he wasn't with them.

She couldn't just walk past them – it would seem too pointed, too deliberate – so she approached them with the look she'd perfected over the years, of professional concern.

Isabelle had a tissue pressed to her face, she was rolling and unrolling it in her hand. As Hannah drew closer she could see threads of pink in the whites of her eyes. 'Ca va?' she ventured. Isabelle shook her head.

'It's Lucy,' Jopi said, in English. 'Apparently she doesn't want to move to Annecy.'

'Not with me, at any rate,' said Isabelle. Her face crumpled, and she blew her nose.

'Really?' Hannah said, 'But I thought—'

'And how does she tell me?' Isabelle burst out. 'By text!' she buried her face in the tissue. 'She wants to move to Lille with that *putain de merde!*'

'Zelie,' Jopi said to Hannah. 'A new artist she has discovered . . .'

'*Artiste de merde!*' said Isabelle. 'She hardly knows her and now she wants to move in with her! Taking her son with her! And we've been together nearly seven years!'

'You should go to her,' Jopi said. 'We can cope.'

'How can I go?' demanded Isabelle. 'I have the whole conference to manage! In any case,' she added bitterly, 'it seems she's made up her mind. Without consulting me!' and she pressed the tissue to her face and wept. Jopi crouched down beside her, making soothing noises.

'Yes, but you have a say in the matter as well,' Karl said. 'I lived with someone once - she had two little boys and do you know, when we broke up that was the most painful bit - losing them?' His face contorted briefly. 'I had no visiting rights - nothing.'

'That must have been difficult,' Heidi said.

'It was!' Karl agreed. 'I still feel the pain, here.' He touched his heart.

Isabelle sobbed even harder.

'You see, it's not just about you,' Heidi said. 'There is the little boy as well - what's his name again?'

'Nico,' Isabelle wept.

'Haven't you looked after him since he was a baby? Just as much as his mother?'

Isabelle nodded, dabbing her eyes with the tissue. 'When

Lucy and Simon broke up, Nico stayed with his father – but at weekends he always came to us – both of us!'

'Well then, there is more than one relationship at stake here,' Heidi said, looking at Hannah for support.

Hannah agreed that Isabelle and Lucy should talk. 'Nothing should be ended by text,' she said.

'Of course not,' Marta said. She added that some time ago, she and her girlfriend had almost split up, and Marta had dropped everything to fly to her in Frankfurt, and here they were, three years later, still together!

'But the conference!' Isabelle cried.

'Marta can help with that,' Jopi said. 'And Pierre and the others – we will all help.'

Isabelle rubbed her nose. 'There's the tour—'

'We can cancel that,' Jopi said, 'or Marta can do it.'

'Sure,' Marta said.

'And the meal—'

'Don't worry about the meal.'

'We'll put up some notices about good places to eat,' Marta said. 'People will make their own arrangements.'

'I, for one, am perfectly happy here,' Heidi said, and Karl said he preferred to explore in any case.

'See?' said Jopi. 'You are not indispensable! And as for the lectures – we will all look after one another. Heidi – you know Giovanna Rossi? She's arriving today – you can show her the theatre and accompany her? Karl, you could stay with Anton, perhaps – and Hannah – could you tell Neville what's happening?'

Hannah felt a twisting sensation in her stomach. 'Oh – I don't think,' she began.

'He's in room 328,' Jopi said, 'just one floor down from you.'

Hannah opened her mouth to say – what? That she had no

intention of going to Neville's room, or of speaking to him again, if she could help it, but Karl said, 'I can tell Neville, I'll be seeing him later in any case.'

'Thank you, Karl,' Jopi said. 'And I will take care of everyone else, so you see, *ma chere Isabelle*, you aren't needed at all!'

'You really should go to Lucy,' Karl said.

Isabelle nodded slowly, then she rose, looking stern and stoic, like a mythical figure of Resolution. Her eyes were glittering.

'Bien,' she said. 'I will go. I will leave immediately.'

'Absolutely,' said Heidi.

'Perfect,' said Jopi, 'And with luck,' she went on, rising rather more awkwardly, 'you will sort things out and return before the conference has ended!'

Jopi and Marta walked Isabelle to the lift, Karl excused himself and set off in a different direction, leaving Heidi with Hannah.

What had Neville said, after she'd left?

But she could hardly ask that. She pulled a sympathetic face then smiled. 'Such a good lecture,' she said, injecting warmth into her voice. 'I thoroughly enjoyed it.'

'Controversial, no?' Heidi said, pleased. 'I thought I would set the fox among the chickens!'

'Cat,' Hannah said. 'Pigeons.'

'It's good to stir things up, yes?'

'Definitely,'

'You want some lunch?'

'Oh,' Hannah said, lifting the bag with the pastries. 'I bought these while I was out. I – have some phone calls to make.'

'Ah, fine,' said Heidi. 'I will see you later – at Giovanna's lecture maybe?'

She didn't wait for a response, but walked away, head lowered, feet turned out, frowning at the floor. Hannah was relieved. She didn't want to commit herself to any more lectures. She glanced across the foyer. Isabelle, Jopi and Marta had already disappeared. Warily, in case Neville stepped out of one, she approached the lifts.

Perhaps she should take the stairs. But her foot hurt.

What was she doing, playing hide and seek?

As the glass lift descended she could see it was empty. She stepped inside, struck by the strangeness of the situation. It almost seemed as though her attempts to avoid Neville were being undermined by some kind of conspiracy to throw them together.

But that was ridiculous, paranoid. She didn't have to go to Neville's room, thank God – Karl had saved her from that particular burden.

Yet there did seem to be something, some kind of energy, moving them towards one another. Like two satellites moving towards collision.

X

HANNAH'S PHONE BEGAN to buzz as she approached her room. She opened the door quickly, taking her phone out of her bag. Thibaut.

'Cherie?' he said. '*Ça va?*'

She felt a rush of emotion so intense she could hardly speak.

'Yes,' she said, in English, her voice shaking, 'I'm here.'

Thibaut switched to English. 'Are you OK?'

'I am now,' she managed.

'You sound a little . . . *distraite.*'

Hannah found she was nodding at the phone. 'I'm OK – are you OK?'

'I'm OK,' he laughed. 'So, we are both OK. How's the conference?'

'Yes, fine. It's been . . . a little tense, that's all.'

She found herself telling him about Isabelle, in more detail than he could possibly want since he didn't know her, while he made listening noises at the other end.

'So, she has left now? But you will manage? Everything's fine?'

'Yes, we'll cope.'

There was a pause. What was wrong with her? Why couldn't she talk to him?

'So, if—' he began, and at the same time she said, 'Thibaut, there's someone here.'

'I should hope so,' he said, teasing. 'It is a conference . . .'

'Someone I knew a long time ago.'

'Yes?' he said, alert.

'From school – primary school. Thibaut – he knew my friend – Joanna.'

'Ah *cherie*—'

'It's fine – I mean – it's just – I think he wants to speak about it, that's all . . .'

'And you do not want to speak about it?'

She shook her head at the phone. 'Not really.'

There was a pause. Thibaut clearly felt he was on uncertain ground.

'Is he – harassing you in some way?'

'N-no . . .'

'You don't seem very sure—'

'It's just – I don't want to talk about it with him—' *Not now, not ever.*

'Can you tell him that? Say it's upsetting for you?'

No. 'I don't know.'

Another pause. 'Do you want me to come and pick you up?'

Yes – more than anything else in the world.

'I don't know – I haven't given my lecture yet.'

'When do you give it?'

'Not till Sunday.'

'Well – but you could postpone it, maybe?'

Hannah shook her head. 'I don't want to let Jopi down – with Isabelle leaving and everything . . .'

'But if this guy is bothering you—'

'It's not that – so much as the memory – of what happened.'

'Sure,' Thibaut said. 'You should tell him that – say it's still painful for you—'

Like that would work.

'Or alternatively—'

'Yes?'

'Sit down with him - let him speak, if there's something he wants to say—'

No, no, no!

'Perhaps he just wants to be heard.'

Most clients, most people, just want to be heard.

'There may be something he has to say that sheds a different light on what happened - that makes you feel better in the end.'

Ah, Thibaut!

'All the years I've known you, you've suffered from this tragedy. You've told me about it, your therapist, the police - but no one else who was directly involved - am I right?'

'Yes, but—'

'Perhaps the same is true for him. And now here you both are, with this unique opportunity - to put the past to rest. I would listen to him, Hannah - hear what he has to say.'

Hannah took the phone away from her ear, stared down at it.

'Hannah?' his voice was distant now.

'Yes?'

'You can talk to him - it's what you do.'

'Yes.'

'But if you don't want to - that's fine too. It's up to you - you don't have to do anything you don't want to do.'

She said nothing.

'Hannah? *Ça va?*'

'Yes.'

'I can't hear you.'

She picked the phone up again. 'I said, yes. I'll think about it.'

'Look – I have to go now – I have the Exam Board in half an hour. But I'll phone you back later – and if you change your mind – if you want me to come and get you – just let me know.'

'Thank you.'

'I mean it, Hannah. Just tell me what you want to do.'

'I love you,' she said. Her voice sounded so remote.

'I love you too. *Je t'aime beaucoup.* Stop worrying – OK? *Il n'y pas le feu au lac.*'

She murmured something in reply. The usual endearments. Then sat, still holding the phone, looking out at the lake. Pearl-coloured, glimmering, merging with the skyline.

There was no fire on the lake. Not that Thibaut knew about, anyway.

But what did Thibaut know?

Only what she'd told him.

XI

THE THINGS THEY found there.

Litter, of course, crushed cans and plastic bottles, cigarette stubs and packets, rubbers. Jo knew what they were but she wouldn't tell Annie. Annie, six months younger, was too young to know, Jo said. And when she finally did tell her, in lurid terms (they pump all this *stuff* into your *hole* and the rubber can burst, like a balloon), Annie was horrified.

Once, they found an old coin, its surface so eroded, blue-green, it was impossible to tell what kind it was. Jo said it was a magic coin, and Annie had to bury it so it would grow into a money tree. She did this, digging her fingers into the wet earth, disturbing some tiny beetles and the tail end of a worm, wriggling frantically.

Jo couldn't do it. Her nails had recently been painted scarlet, like her mother's, although they were already chipped.

Annie finished burying the coin and stood up, wiping her fingers on her skirt.

'Now what?' she said.

'Now you walk around it three times, widdershins, saying a rhyme.'

There was some argument about why Annie had to say the rhyme (because she'd buried it), and which direction widdershins was, but in the end Annie circled the spot in an anti-clockwise direction saying, 'Money tree, grow for me,' while Jo watched from a fallen trunk. Part of it was sculpted out and moss-covered, like a seat, and Jo sat there, like the queen of the forest. She watched Annie skipping solemnly around the little patch of disturbed earth, and covered her mouth as though trying not to laugh. Annie knew what she was doing, she even played up to it, flinging one arm out and declaiming to the sky, *Money tree, grow for me!*

When Jo had enough she stood up saying, 'Now follow me!'

And Annie always did.

The ground was uneven, sloping, with dips and rises, leading to crevices. Trees bristled on their flanks, leaning over at impossible angles, one almost perpendicular to the slope. There was mud at the bottom that turned into a stream when it rained.

Annie hurried after Jo, panting, sweating, saying they should leave now, go back home, her mother might be back.

'Go on then!' Jo always said. It was understood by both of them that Jo didn't need Annie. Jo would be happy to play in the Wild on her own, so Annie could go. But she never did. She was hampered by the sense that she couldn't navigate the Wild on her own, but also she didn't want to leave. More obscurely, she felt that the Wild wouldn't let her go.

It was magic, Jo said, and Annie believed her. When the wind blew, it did seem to be possessed by a glad spirit, putting everything in motion.

At other times it was dappled and mysterious. Islands of light swam between trees, the sun deposited long shadows across the path. Or it was brooding and solemn, with an unearthly stillness. The trees' shadows sank into dark pools on the ground, a latticework of roots poked through the path like bones. Even the occasional bird call seemed far away.

A long way in, there was a wall. Or part of a wall ending in a tumble of stones, sand-coloured, veined, with splotches of moss growing over them, and ferns sprouting between.

This wall was the Boundary, Jo said, where the human world ended and the Fairy world began. Annie believed this as well. Beyond the wall, the Wild did become more entangled, mysterious. One thing shifted rapidly into another in the half-light.

There was a fallen trunk, with two holes like eyes and a shock of thin branches sprouting upwards like hair. Another tree had pale bark stippled with what looked like the claw marks of birds; its branches were outspread like arms.

There were trees that grew twisted together, and others that had trunks draped like the folds of a gown, the hems studded with dandelions, or bluebells.

They used to be fairy queens, Jo said. At midnight, at full moon, they would dance together.

More than anything, Annie wanted to see that. But Jo said most of the fairies had gone now, they had moved away long ago. Or they had changed slowly over the years, back into their natural state: trees, or owls. The ones that were left were not beautiful, like real fairies, but hideously ugly. Joanna called them the Others.

The Others didn't want to be seen, Jo said. They were good at hiding. If they thought they'd been seen they would shoot elf-bolts at you, or sting you with poison ivy. They would bind you with spider-threads strong as silk and carry you to their lair.

That was why you had to move quickly to see one, and even faster to get away. Annie was never quick enough. And she was clumsy - the Others would hear her coming from miles off. So she didn't see one, although she often thought she had seen something, moving quickly, furtively, between thickets. In some places the bracken was trampled, and once they found ribs of wood stacked into a barricade. That proved the Others had been there. They would use the barricades to shelter from humans, or to hide behind when they fired their darts.

Sometimes Annie would find an eggshell, blue, pecked open, or the whorled shell of a snail. That was what the Others ate, Jo said, baby birds and snails.

One time they found actual bones. Jo said they were the bones of a dead baby. The Others took them, she said. The ones that lived didn't get any older, but they had wrinkled old faces like goblins. Some of them didn't thrive (Jo's mother was a midwife) and when they died the Others buried them out here.

Another time, they found a wire on a spring. Annie thought it was a trap for animals, but Jo said it was how the Others caught human children. She said if Annie touched it, it would snap tight around her hand and drag her down into the earth.

On the track that led to the reservoir there was a strange metallic construction. It looked like a drill or some kind of winding mechanism going into the ground. The earth around it smelled of rust.

It had a small wheel that neither of them could turn. But if you could turn it, Jo said, it would open up a passage that led down into the dungeons of a castle. There you might meet the Watchman. The Watchman had a scarred face and one milky eye. He would come after you in your dreams, you would hear the clump-clump-clump of his boots.

Another time, she said it was what was left of a gate to the Underworld. Also it was Barley when they played hide and seek; it was whatever she said it was.

Once they passed this, they could slide down the bank to the water, dislodging hundreds of tiny stones.

On the far side of the reservoir a small platform jutted out into the water, its wooden planks rotting and broken. To get to it you had to cross a bank that was stippled with stones, like a stony beach. Some were large and flat and mossy, others little more than pebbles. One of Jo and Annie's games was to try to reach the platform without getting their feet wet, by stepping on the stones. Jo leapt easily from one to another, while Annie moved much more cautiously, falling behind.

The water was very still, but sometimes there would be the merest wrinkling of the surface, as if something was moving beneath it. That was the Others, Jo said. Some of them lurked beneath the water, waiting to drag humans down into the depths. If you lay on a stone and looked into the water, you might see a girl's face looking up, mouth opening and closing like a fish. That was one of the Drowned Girls. Jo said she'd seen one, but Annie was never quick enough.

If you disturbed them, they would rise to the surface, Jo said. When the rains fell and the reservoir swelled beyond its banks, all the Drowned Girls would rush out in a stream.

Annie did, and didn't want to see the Drowned Girls, in the same way as she did and didn't want to see the Others. It was part of the game to go into the water without disturbing them. Greatly daring, they would take off their trainers and socks and paddle in the shallow bits where the pebbles were smaller and dug into the soles of their feet. Or they would find a large stone to lie on and blow bubbles through reeds into the still depths. Then they could see into that upside-down country, where the Others lived. If you listened hard, you could hear them doing their washing, beating wrinkled cloths on stone. Sometimes Jo would see one, and then they would scramble back over the stones, as fast as they could. Hannah never saw one. Sometimes she would get tired of the game and lie on her back instead, squinting at the sun, smelling the sweet scent of decay, listening to the trilling of birds that were just out of sight.

At tea-time, meaty smells came from the houses, telling them it was time to go home, but they never wanted to leave.

Neither of them was supposed to play in The Wild, it was too dangerous. A boy had drowned there, years ago, and another had broken his leg. Gangs of youths, teenagers from the college, would make their way there, and to them Hannah's mother attributed drug-taking and murderous intent. Or other, murkier desires that were never named.

'Stay in, stay home, stay safe,' she commanded.

But Annie didn't want to stay at home.

Home was fish paste sandwiches and boiled mince. It was her mother hoovering savagely, working herself into an apocalyptic rage. It was looking out onto wet rooves, and blank windows, and pavements where pools of water collected in the cracks. It was waiting in the corner shop while Mr Owen served all the adults first, and then taking home the wrong thing, or nothing, because he'd run out. It was coughs and colds and ear infections, veruccas and the smell of Vicks. School was suppressing the answers you knew, because being clever was the worst crime of all, and in PE, trying to hide the holes in your vest and socks.

So although her mother told her she wasn't to see Jo again, she had to stay in, Annie just waited until her mother, always busy, always preoccupied, couldn't be bothered any more. Or had to go to work. Then Annie would lift the latch on the back gate and run along the narrow alley which led to the path at the back of Jo's garden and wait. If Jo wanted to see her she would raise the blind at her window. If it was fully lowered she might have to stay in, do homework or help in the house.

If it was half-raised, she might have another friend round. On those occasions Annie would wait for a long time, hoping the blind would lift. If it didn't, she would return home slowly, dragging her steps, feeling as though all the light and colour had drained from the day.

XII

LATER, HANNAH HAD hardly any memory of how she got to Neville's room.

The doors were featureless, with a bronze gleam, the number barely visible on the black card-key holder to one side. 328 was the sixth door she came to, although she couldn't remember counting.

But as she stood in front of it, she felt a rush of horror that made her mouth turn dry, her flesh shrink.

What was she doing?

Was she really going to knock on his door?

She was startled by a noise, but it was two women at the far end of the corridor, talking animatedly.

She was aware of her heart pumping erratically. Her breathing had a ragged quality, catching on the in-breath.

Before she could change her mind she tapped on the door. And then again, more incisively.

In the seconds that followed, many scenarios rushed through her mind. Collapsing slowly into the realisation that no one had answered.

He wasn't there.

She lifted up her hand again, knocked more slowly. 'Neville?' she managed to say. It came out primly, with a slight quaver, not as she intended.

Nothing.

Relief turned her limbs to water; she felt as though she

might collapse against the door. Later, she would remember leaning against it for a moment, pressing her fingertips to the smooth surface, and closing her eyes. In fact, she stepped away.

She could smell sweat leaking from her. She was in no state to see anyone now – what was she thinking?

She'd thought she would do as Thibaut had suggested. *Just listen to him, Hannah, hear what he has to say.*

But he wasn't there.

If she believed in Divine Providence, which she didn't, then Neville's absence would surely be an example of it. The message the universe was trying to communicate to her couldn't be any clearer. She wasn't meant to have any kind of conversation with Neville, confrontational or otherwise. She should leave.

Should she write a note, as he'd done? Push it under the door?

No. She didn't want him to reply. And in any case, she didn't have any paper with her. She turned towards the lift, then changing her mind (what if he got out of it?) veered towards the stairs. It was only one flight to her room. Her speed accelerated as she approached her own door. She fumbled for her card almost dropping her bag, then let herself in, grateful for the cool olive light, the door locking behind her. She went towards her bed, but instead of lying on it, sank down on her knees at its side, like a child saying prayers, and covered her face briefly with her hands.

I tried, Thibaut, she thought.

When she lifted her face again she could see the lake through the hotel window, its polished sheen freckled with light.

It had been years before she could look at a lake, or any stretch of water, without feeling sick and dizzy. She would go out of her way to avoid even a pond.

v many nights had she woken gasping from dreams in
Drowned Girls slapped like fish against her window?
ty years ago, there had been practically no therapeutic
or children. It had been one of the things she'd fought
for in her career, to establish some kind of service for every
child in every school. How many children had she helped –
children suffering from physical or emotional abuse, from drug
addicted, violent or unstable parents who should never (in her
private conviction) have had them?

She'd come a long way in her own life without that help.
She'd gone to grammar school, then university, pursued her
chosen career. She'd left the small northern town she'd grown
up in and never returned. Now she lived here, in Switzerland,
where there was water everywhere, as though the past had no
hold over her at all.

But because of Neville, she was being sucked back into it,
dragged under like a Drowned Girl.

She wouldn't let it happen.

She wasn't going to talk to him.

Thibaut was wrong, on this occasion at least.

She'd told Thibaut not to come and pick her up. If she
changed her mind now he'd want to know why. He would ask
questions she didn't want to answer, so she was stuck here.
She would have to spend the next two days avoiding Neville
somehow.

That evening, probably, he would go out to eat with Jopi
and the rest. They might invite Hannah to join them. But
she'd already decided to visit the Old Town. Last year she'd
found a good vegetarian restaurant there, and had eaten
alone. She couldn't remember the name, but she could remember roughly where it was. If she set off early she could
avoid everyone, and spend the evening wandering around

the Old Town, which was her favourite part of Geneva.

An hour later she had showered, then dressed again in her casual clothes; same trousers and linen shirt, different T-shirt. She clipped her hair back, applied lipstick, set off walking briskly from her room.

The afternoon was passing imperceptibly into evening. The lake reflected a pastel light. Fortunately, the conference centre was on the same side as the Old Town - Hannah didn't have to cross the Mont Blanc Bridge where tourists were already swarming. She crossed the main road instead and began the ascent towards the cathedral.

It was surrounded by tourists, Japanese students, elderly American couples. Artists plied their work outside; there was a balalaika player and an accordionist. Stalls selling crepes and waffles, keyrings, postcards. Hannah wove between them, and entered a web of streets too narrow for the number of tourists surging through. Already she was beginning to think she'd made a mistake. Why hadn't she stayed in her room and sent for food?

In the course of her professional training, Hannah had discovered that she had a developmental co-ordination disorder called dyspraxia. This diagnosis had explained many things to her: why she was no good at PE; why she always lost her kit when she went swimming; why she still, despite nearly a hundred lessons, couldn't drive. It meant that she had virtually no recognition of place, no ability to hold maps or directions in her mind, would regularly turn left instead of right.

The mind maps out personality using memory and place: this was where that happened; this happened here. The dyspraxic child is more than usually co-dependent, not only needing a sense of direction from others, but a sense of who they are.

Of course, other people were likely to consider them stupid or inadequate, and they accept this, as very young children accept the strangeness of the world. The criminal justice system is full of dyspraxic children, who have simply followed others around.

It had taken some time for Hannah to understand why she'd simply done everything Joanna had told her to, and followed her everywhere.

Over the years she'd developed strategies to overcome her disorder: memorising landmarks, counting steps, developing a hyper-awareness of time – sixteen minutes to walk from her house to the Place de Gare, eleven to the shops. Professionally, she was known for being severely punctual, meticulously organised. OCD, her less charitable colleagues said. Now she remembered that last year it had taken her six minutes to walk from the cathedral to the vegetarian restaurant, and that she'd kept the Cathedral to her right, but still she couldn't seem to find it. There was no one to ask, everyone she saw looked like a tourist. She felt a familiar surge of desolation and hopelessness.

She passed several galleries, a small market, a restaurant that looked like a chalet, that she knew to be ferociously expensive, another one that looked as if it only served fish, then the Chocolaterie Tea room with its red umbrellas outside, that told her she was in the old cattle market, the Place Bourg-de-four.

Finally she found, not the restaurant she'd been looking for, but another one, in the Rue des Voisins. An unprepossessing shop front, but a pretty garden to the rear, with vine-covered trellises around the tables. Gratefully she sank down and ordered wine.

As soon as it came, she began to relax. She was no one

here, after all, there was nothing to identify her, a middle-aged woman, nondescript, unobtrusive, partially obscured by vines. She could watch the rest of the world passing by.

On the other side of the vines there was a young woman with a scarlet neckerchief, playing Haydn sonatas on a violin. Three older women wheeled suitcases along the pavement, a man with a pushchair extended his phone towards a medieval tower on the other side of the square. Two teenage boys whizzed by on scooters, rap blaring from some kind of box. Hannah leaned back in her seat. For the first time since coming to the conference, she felt invisible, at ease. She could stay here as long as she liked. Who would notice or care?

The food, when it arrived, was excellent; stuffed aubergines, their oily interiors smelling of rosemary and oregano, a creamy butternut squash risotto, crusty bread. Hannah ate almost angrily, as though starving, drank half a bottle of good wine, considered ordering more.

The girl in the red neckerchief began to pack up her violin, taking the coins out of a bowler hat. Hannah saw she was etched all over with tattoos. There was webbing up her forearm that reminded Hannah sharply of one of her former clients, a young girl called Louisa, or Lou.

Lou was fourteen, self-contained, incommunicative. Covered in tattoos that weren't professionally etched, like the young violinist's. She'd inked them herself, using a pin and some antiseptic lotion.

'She's crazy about spiders,' her mother had said sourly. And indeed, a spiders' web covered one half of her face, there was another across her chest and more along her arms. Her hair was dyed jet black (both parents were blonde) she had black eyeliner and purple lips.

This in itself wouldn't be a reason for treatment, although

some of the tattoos were scabbed, the outlines flaming red, and she'd been taken to hospital after attempting to inject dye into her eyelids as a permanent liner. Lou was obviously a Goth, like many other teenagers.

Only in this case she had her own personal demon, called Hetta. She'd been referred by her distraught parents after she'd disembowelled the family dog, in an attempt to read the future from his entrails.

Haruspicy. Normally performed by a haruspex.

'That's what I am,' she'd said.

'You're a haruspex?' Hannah asked.

Lou nodded.

'How do you know this?'

'I was told.'

'By?'

But Lou would rarely say her name, so Hannah said it for her. 'Hetta?'

Lou nodded again, soot-black hair falling forward. Why was it so difficult to get a natural-looking black from hair dye?

Lou probably wouldn't have wanted natural black.

'Hetta told you you're a haruspex?'

More nodding.

'And what does that involve?'

Lou mumbled something and Hannah had to ask her to repeat it.

'Divining stuff, and that.'

'You mean, the future?'

Lou started to nod, then shook her head. 'Divining her Will.'

'You mean – what she wants you to do?'

Nodding.

'But I thought she told you what to do?'

Lou sighed, muttered to herself. Then she said, 'There's more to it than that. There's what's said, and what's not said.'

True enough, Hannah thought.

'So, you have to interpret Hetta?'

A single nod.

'And – what kinds of things does she want you to do?'

Mainly, it seemed, she wanted Lou to knit. She'd knitted, and crocheted, vast webs across her room. Sometimes she brought wool with her, to the sessions. She knitted viciously, pulling the yarn so tightly around her thumb that the tip of it was white. She'd knitted a black top in the pattern of a web and wore it over a vest.

'Does Hetta like webs?'

No answer.

'Why do you think she wants you to knit them?'

No answer.

'Does she live in them?'

Muffled snort. 'She int a spider!'

'No? But why does she need all these webs?'

Silence.

'Have you ever seen her?'

Nothing.

'Does she look like a spider?'

A brief, scarcely perceptible, shake of the head.

'What does she look like?'

Lou peeked from her hair, eyes glinting like sickle moons. 'Like Evil.'

'Really? What does that look like?'

'Just – evil.'

'I'm finding that a little hard to imagine. Does she look like anyone I might know? From TV for instance?'

Lou sighed.

'Perhaps you're not supposed to say?'

Silence. Was that assent? A thought occurred to Hannah. 'Could you draw her?'

More silence, but Hannah was always equipped with materials. She passed Lou a drawing pad and pencils. Lou didn't take them.

'I have pens, or paints if you prefer?'

After a long moment, Lou took the pad.

Hannah waited while Lou sketched, slowly at first then with more confidence. She took her time over it, covering most of the A4 pad. Her mother had said the only subject she really liked at school was art.

Hannah noted her absorption. She thought Lou's eyes might actually be closed but it was hard to tell. She didn't look up, didn't pause. Perhaps fifteen minutes went by before she stopped, letting the pad droop on her knee.

'Have you finished now? Is that Hetta?'

Lou didn't reply.

'Do you mind if I look?'

No response. Hannah got up and stood behind Lou, without taking the pad from her.

Although she didn't remember Lou looking at her even once in the course of their session, there was a passable portrait of Hannah on the pad.

She'd re-told this story, omitting Lou's name, to Thibaut, and in lectures, to people who'd found it funny. But remembering it now, she felt the same disturbed qualm as she'd felt then.

She was unsettled, that was all, dislocated. Her body was reacting exactly as it had when she'd seen the drawing. But she wasn't *there*, in an office in England with a young client. She was here, in a restaurant in Geneva's Old Town.

And she should probably be getting back to the Conference Centre. Unless she made her way to the station, caught the train to Lucerne. She could be home before midnight.

But of course, she wouldn't do that. She would do what was expected of her. She took a final sip of wine, dabbed her mouth on the napkin, left a decent tip.

Soon she was lost again. Following one meandering group of tourists after another. She passed an art gallery, a jewellers, several shops selling models of Swiss chalets and cuckoo clocks. There was an elderly man in lederhosen in front of one chalet, and a young girl in a checked skirt, with two goats. Heidi, of course.

Then Hannah saw a model of Old Geneva in a narrow window. It was the medieval town, with none of the modern landmarks, but she examined it anyway, hoping it might help her to navigate.

It had been rendered in loving detail. The houses had shutters at the windows. No gardens, but tiny window boxes full of flowers. There was a well, and a man driving a cart, his horse was chewing hay. The cathedral had a tower with a bell, and there was a cobbled street leading to the market-place.

'You might almost expect to see the two of us down there,' Neville said, over her shoulder.

Hannah jerked away from him, pressing her hand to her chest.

'Oh dear,' Neville said. 'I'm so sorry! I didn't mean to startle you.'

Hannah couldn't speak.

'Me and my clumsy ways,' he continued. 'I just don't think.'

'It's fine,' Hannah managed. She flinched away from him, as he moved, in case he touched her.

'Well, now that I've scared you half to death,' he said, 'I

should say that we were hoping you might accompany us?' He gestured towards the end of the alley, where, Hannah now saw, Karl stood with another young man. She felt a twinge of relief that he wasn't alone, she wasn't alone with him.

Karl waved enthusiastically but the young man didn't move. He had finely chiselled features and dreadlocks. Senegalese, she guessed.

'Have you met Anton yet?' Neville continued. 'He's giving the lecture before yours. We've just been out and about, exploring the Old Town, and now we're looking for someplace to eat. We would love you to join us.'

'Thank you – I've eaten,' Hannah said, sounding too severe. She tried to smile.

'Oh – but you could still join us for a drink?'

'I'm . . . a bit tired. I thought I'd better get back, for an early night.'

'Conferences are wearing,' Neville agreed. 'but if you want to go *back*, you're heading in the wrong direction.' He nodded towards the opposite end of the square.

'Oh, really? I must have taken a wrong turn.'

'You're sure you won't join us? Karl and Anton will be so disappointed.'

Hannah glanced at them. They had turned away, Karl was gesticulating towards something Hannah couldn't see. 'I'm sorry,' she said.

'Was it good?'

'What?'

'The restaurant? You don't eat meat either, I believe. Is it near?'

'Er – I – yes,' she said, realising at the same time she couldn't remember the name. Or location. 'It was over there,' she gestured vaguely.

Neville copied her. 'Just - over there?' he said. Then he smiled. 'You never did have a sense of direction, as I recall.'

To her annoyance, Hannah felt herself blushing. 'No, well,' she mumbled, turning away, wondering how she could end this conversation. Surely he would give up soon?

'Did you get my note?'

Hannah's heart started knocking again.

'I did,' she said, turning back to him. 'Since you pushed it under my door.'

'Ah - yes - I hope you don't mind - I was so afraid I might miss you - and we wouldn't get a chance to catch up.'

How did you get my room number? Hannah wanted to say. Was that too accusatory?

'Did Jopi give you my room number?' she asked.

'What? Oh, no - it was one of the helpers - François, I think. They have a complete list. And I told him we're old friends.' He smiled his yellow smile. *Surely that was a breach of security,* Hannah thought, she should mention it to Jopi. Neville was still smiling genially, blinking at her. She gave him the look that had always worked well in Board meetings, or when dealing with management, but Neville seemed immune.

'You didn't answer it,' he said, 'the note.'

Hannah held the pause a little longer than usual. Then she said, 'I tried. I called by your room. I knocked.'

'That was *you*?'

'You were there?'

'You woke me up,' he said. 'I'd fallen asleep. Then I thought I heard someone knocking - but by the time I answered the door, you'd gone.'

Why didn't she believe him? 'I'm sorry if I disturbed you,' she said.

'Oh no - don't be - it's a bad habit - sleeping in the

afternoons. Very elderly.' He grinned at her wolfishly. 'You should have knocked again,' he said.

Hannah stared at him.

'Well,' he said. 'What were you going to say?'

Hannah looked at him blankly. He said, 'Were you going to accept my invitation?'

'I—' Hannah said, but Neville interrupted her, 'I'd be delighted if you would – these conferences fly by, and in no time at all everyone's leaving, and it might be another forty years before we meet up again.'

He smiled his unnerving smile.

All at once, a sense of weariness washed over Hannah. She was tired of fighting, of resisting him. *Just listen to what he has to say.*

'Yes,' she said. 'Why not?'

'Wonderful!' Neville said. 'I checked the menu in the Bistro – there's a salad plate, and mezze that both come without meat, unusually. Have you noticed how *salad* in Switzerland often means cold meat or sausage?'

Hannah wondered how she could make her escape.

'And there's vegetable soup as well,' Neville said. 'With croutons. I do so love croutons, don't you? In any case, there's plenty of choice.' He beamed as though he'd arranged it specially himself.

I could invite Jopi, Hannah thought suddenly. *And Heidi.*

'The others are all going out, by the way – on that boat tour. Marta's organising it while Isabelle's away. So it'll just be the two of us.'

Hannah turned away again, shaking her head slightly, as if to herself.

'But there'll be so much to say!' Neville cried, gaily. 'After all these *years!*'

Hannah glanced towards Karl and Anton, who were looking at them now. Karl grinned and lifted his hand again.

'So much that *couldn't* be said, in the circumstances.'

Hannah turned back to him sharply.

'Only if you want to,' he added hastily. 'Some things probably shouldn't be said, after all. I'm all for letting sleeping dogs lie . . .'

'What do you *want*, Neville?' Hannah said abruptly. Neville's eyes grew round. 'Oh, oh *dear*,' he said in alarm. 'I didn't mean to . . . I mean . . .'

He trailed off, helplessly. But there was that look in his eyes. Hannah regretted agreeing to meet him. She stared at him, pouring all the intensity of her aversion into her glare.

'I only meant it'll be really good to catch up, that's all! You know what?' he said, 'We don't have to talk about anything if you don't want to – it'll just be a pleasure to have lunch with you. *You* can choose what we talk about,' he said.

Hannah could feel her stare turning cold. 'Your friends are waiting,' she said, nodding towards them.

'They *are*,' exclaimed Neville, as though this had just occurred to him. 'Well – and you're sure you won't join us – just for one little drink?'

But Hannah stepped away, in what she hoped was the right direction this time. She lifted a hand to Karl and Anton.

'I'll say you're tired, shall I?' Neville said. When she didn't respond, he raised his voice, calling after her. 'See you tomorrow then, after the lecture – *in the bistro!*'

XIII

HANNAH PUSHED HER way through the narrow streets, the crowds of tourists. Her pace was at odds with theirs, faster. By the time she passed the Cathedral she was almost running.

Why had she agreed to meet him?

Now she would have to go to his lecture. And miss Dr Abimbola's – the one she'd really wanted to attend.

She should have gone with the three of them for a drink. Safety in numbers. Neville couldn't accuse her of avoiding him then.

What did he want to talk about?

Karl and Anton would probably think she was rude.

She was used to that – she had a reputation for being anti-social. Something about her seemed to chill people, prevent them from making overtures.

Apart from Neville, of course.

At work they thought of her as efficient, hard-working, unapproachable. She always stayed after hours, never went for lunch with her colleagues or for drinks, was never tempted to stray beyond a professional relationship into friendship. Even Jopi, whom she liked, who always invited her to speak at these conferences, she wouldn't class as a *friend*, exactly. She knew little about her, they didn't share personal confidences.

It was probably true to say Thibaut was her only friend.

Sometimes she and Thibaut were invited out together, as

a couple. Usually Hannah would be working, and Thibaut would go on his own. That was probably a relief, for whoever had invited them.

Everyone liked Thibaut. She felt the familiar wave of disbelief that he had chosen her.

Thibaut would think it was a good thing that she'd agreed to meet Neville for lunch.

Without thinking about it, Hannah had left the Old Town. It took her a moment to realise she was facing the Mont Blanc Bridge.

She didn't have to cross it to get back to the conference centre, but she paused anyway, looking at the lanes of traffic, the flags along its railings.

For years, Hannah wouldn't cross any bridge that ran over water. But then she'd come here, to live in this country of lakes. It had taken her six years to agree to the move. There was no question of Thibaut moving; he loved his job, his home. And in any case, Hannah wanted to move. She wanted a new start.

She didn't tell anyone about her fear of water. Everyone knew phobias were rooted in childhood. She could have lied, of course, talked about some trauma in the swimming pool. But instead, she'd adopted a systematic, willed approach to overcoming her fear; looking at images of water, then approaching small streams or ponds, walking on paths that went near but not too near a river, trying her first short bridge.

The Mont Blanc bridge was 250 metres long. Long for a bridge, but not long in real terms. At a normal pace it would take her three minutes to cross. Less if she jogged, of course, but she wouldn't jog. She would force herself to walk normally, practise her breathing. She would just go a little way, then return.

You've not got it in you, her mother's voice said.

All her nerves were jangling, her lips felt numb. Ridiculous. Hannah pressed herself towards the bridge, head slightly lowered as if preparing to charge.

Once she was on it she didn't look at the railings, through which the water pitched and swayed.

Her mother, who wouldn't step on a plane, would never have visited, had been another good reason for moving to Switzerland. Although, in fact, she'd died a few months before Hannah had moved. There were no other ties keeping her in England, she could leave everything behind. Which was what she wanted. She'd already changed her life by moving to University, then to Bristol for her first job. It wasn't enough. She still wanted a new start, in a new country, where she would change her name by marriage. Where no one had heard of Annie Price, or Jo Pearson.

Already she had the sensation that the bridge was moving beneath her, shifting, becoming less solid. It wasn't possible, of course, but still there was a sheen of sweat on her upper lip.

People were glancing at her. She was swaying a little as though drunk, moving in a not quite straight line. The fluid in her inner ears must have shifted in response, not to sensory input – the bridge wasn't actually moving, but to some mechanism in her brain that told her it was. She was veering towards the railings. She gripped the nearest one.

She could see the Jet d'Eau, a plume of light against the evening sky. Pumping 500 litres of water a second, to a height of 140 metres.

So much water, like a geyser, but man made. It made her throat ache, bile rise from her stomach. She clutched another railing with her other hand. When she closed her eyes she had the sensation of falling over the side, arms and legs flailing.

She could see, vividly, the black gape of Jo's mouth surfacing, then sinking again into the green water.

Here she was, the keynote speaker at an international conference, clinging to railings with her eyes shut.

She could hear the girls in her class singing,

Annie Price, She's not nice, She's got lice, She eats mice . . .

Jo would be leading them. She would never play with Hannah at school, although everyone knew they played together in the Wild. If anyone accused her of it, she would deny it.

Eww, she would say. *I wouldn't play with* her.

If they had to sit together, because their surnames both began with a 'P', Jo would draw her things away from Annie's ostentatiously.

For some reason, the other children couldn't cope with the two names, Hannah and Joanna, being so similar. They'd become Annie and Jo. Or, more usually, Jo and Annie. Joanna hated that.

It's Joanna, she would insist, her face flushed with frustration. *Not Jo! Get that through your thick heads, can't you?*

Hannah could hear her voice so clearly, as if the forty years since she'd last heard it hadn't happened. She knew that stress could blur the distinctions in the mind, between *now* and *then*; between sensory input and the interpretation of that input. The bridge wasn't actually moving, it was solid, and strong. She wasn't in the past, she was here, now.

Hannah opened her eyes.

There was the fountain, erupting from the lake. Behind it was an array of buildings. The sky had deepened to a royal blue, and the buildings shed lights like electric ribbons in the lake. Between Hannah and the fountain there was only water, liquid shadows moving across it, mountains, and buildings shimmering and shifting in its depths.

It was 310 metres to the bottom.

The psychologist, William James, had said consciousness was like a glass-bottomed boat, floating on a lake. It was only possible to see what was directly below the boat; the problem was getting the boat to move, so you could see more of the lake.

Memories are stored in the tangled depths. They begin as electrical impulses in the brain, travelling through the hippocampus to the cortex. The process of storage appears to be random. There are 86 billion neurons in the brain. The chance of something being stored in the cortex, and then accessing it again is tiny.

I *don't remember*, Hannah had said, over and over again, I *didn't see*.

Once, Joanna's mother had stopped Hannah in the street, clasping her face in her hands. 'You must know,' she'd said, her head nodding, shaking, 'please, tell me.' Hannah's mother had intervened. 'Leave the child alone,' she'd said, staring at Joanna's mother with those mad, pale eyes. 'D'you not think she's had enough questioning?'

Only Hannah's mother could have made Joanna's mother step backwards, her hands dropping uselessly to her sides. Hannah could feel her watching them as they walked away. Once they were home, Hannah's mother said nothing more about it. She barely spoke to Hannah at all about *the incident*, then, or at any other time.

But she had leapt to Hannah's defence.

It was the one time Hannah thought that maybe she could have talked to her, told her what had really happened, in the hope that her mother would still have defended her, have told her how to think about it, what to say.

Thankfully, she hadn't given in to that impulse. She would

have had to trust her mother completely. She couldn't do that.
It was Joanna who'd taught her, systematically, not to trust.

XIV

HANNAH WOKE FROM a dream in which she was searching for the lecture theatre along one corridor after another. They looked like the corridors in her old school, identical doors, scratched blue paint, opening onto classrooms. When she opened the right door, finally, there was Joanna, with her mother. They were sitting together on a settee, holding hands.

When she woke, she remained still for several moments, staring at the wall.

Neville, she thought. It was the day of his lecture. And she'd agreed to have lunch with him.

The dumb weight of the dream seemed to be pulling her down with its own gravitational force. Already she could feel a headache coming on.

Was Joanna's mother dead now too?

There was no reason why she should be. She'd had her children young, although Hannah hadn't realised that at the time. Now she would be eighty, perhaps, but still. Hannah's own mother had died relatively early, of heart failure, but there was no reason to think Mrs Pearson, as Hannah had always known her, had also died.

But in the dream, she and Joanna had been sitting together, holding hands, looking at Hannah. There were weeds in Joanna's hair.

With a sudden energy, Hannah pushed the bedclothes back.

She was overthinking it, that was always her problem. No psychotherapist would have difficulty in interpreting her dream as the offshoot of anxiety about Neville.

She did some stretching, had another shower. Dressed in the navy suit and cream shirt, combed her hair into a chignon, considered the programme. Neville's lecture was in less than an hour.

What if he spoke about her? About what had happened in their childhood?

Of course he would. That was why he wanted Hannah to be there, to expose her, show her up.

Ridiculous. Surely he would talk about his professional research?

But he might mention what had happened, draw on it.

If he did, there was nothing she could do about it.

It would be better to know.

She thought about going down to breakfast, but she wasn't hungry. And she didn't want to see anyone. She could have coffee in her room.

Coffee, and perhaps a quick walk, for some air.

Then Neville's lecture.

Neville bumped into the chair put out for him, apologised to no one in particular, then knocked the desk. He shuffled some papers, spent an inordinate amount of time fiddling with the control panel. The screen flickered on, then off, then a series of images scrolled past too rapidly to see. Finally, one of the volunteers, François? leapt forward to help. But at the same time something worked and the screen image stilled.

A picture of Adam and Eve. The famous one, by Durer, with the fig leaves, the snake coiling suggestively above Eve's hand.

'Right,' Neville said. 'Here we are.' He leaned over his notes again. The screen went blank.

The lecture theatre was approximately one third full. Presumably, everyone else had gone to Dr Abimbola's lecture. That was why Jopi wasn't there. Hannah couldn't see Heidi, Karl or Anton yet, but there was still time for people to arrive.

She'd chosen a seat on the back row again, near an exit. Poised for flight, although she could hardly run out, that would be too conspicuous. Already a sensation of discomfort had spread from her hips to her spine. She shifted, attempted to cross her legs, then uncrossed them. No room.

A troop of younger delegates arrived, filing in near the front. Then an older woman hurried to a seat.

Neville glanced around. Ridiculously, Hannah felt an impulse to hide. But he didn't seem to be looking for her. He fiddled with the controls again, and the screen leapt to life once more. Adam and Eve.

'I was always taught to begin at the beginning,' he said, and there was a small ripple of laughter. Followed by a second one, when the subheading EVE DID IT drifted into place beneath the image.

He waited while another delegate found a seat, then began.

'So, this is one of our oldest stories,' he said, 'A key one, fundamental to three of the world's major religions. I'm assuming you know it.'

More laughter. Already the audience liked him; they were relaxing into his lecture, expecting to be entertained. Hannah's leg began to jiggle but she stopped it.

'Basically, it's about shame, and blame. And punishment of course – let's not forget that—'

Another famous image, of Adam and Eve being expelled from the Garden.

'You all know how it goes,' Neville continued, 'Eve's tempted by the serpent, she bites the apple, offers it to Adam. God is hacked off.'

He began to read: 'Unto the woman, he said, I will greatly multiply thy sorrow . . .'

The man with the horn-rimmed glasses, who'd sat in front of Hannah in Heidi's lecture, advanced slowly up the stairs towards her. *Seriously?* she thought as he paused by her row. She sighed pointedly, picked up her bag, stood to one side. He sat only three seats away from her. Hannah sat down again, angling herself away from him.

'—cursed is the ground for thy sake; in sorrow shalt thou eat of it all the days of thy life.

'Thorns also and thistles shall it bring forth to thee; and thou shalt eat the herb of the field; In the sweat of thy face shalt thou eat bread, till thou return unto the ground; for dust thou art, and unto dust shalt thou return.'

Hannah shifted once more in her seat. Why were lecture seats so uniformly uncomfortable?

'A bit harsh, really,' Neville continued, 'for eating an apple. And the serpent doesn't get away with it either – he has to crawl on his belly and eat dust. Big emphasis on eating in this story – I'd like us to note that. But also, I'd like us to consider just how much of the Old Testament, which, as I say, is the basis of three major religions, is concerned with judgement, rule-making and breaking, and punishment.'

Several images appeared successively on the screen, Lot's wife, Jonah and the Whale, the Angel of Death visiting the Egyptians.

Hannah opened her bag, extracting a notebook from it, and checked on her room key. There it was, in the zipped compartment. Hannah closed her bag. She couldn't leave yet.

'Obviously there are other stories, testing stories, Job, Abraham and Isaac, forgiveness stories, the prodigal son – but I think it's fair to say that a major part of the Old Testament is concerned with Crime and Punishment, to quote the title of another famous book.

'So I want to leave that with you, while we take a look at these fellows here . . .'

A grainy, black and white image of three shapes in a tank, appeared.

'These little beauties are octopuses. They were given names by the guy who worked with them – Peter Dews. He called them Albert, Bertram and Charles. Now, unfortunately, I don't have any original footage, but the same experiments have been repeated many times. And what happens is this.'

The screen showed a YouTube clip of a scuba diver descending towards an octopus who reached out a tentacle to explore him in a friendly, curious way. Then, in another clip, an octopus learned how to unscrew a jar to obtain food. Finally, an octopus and a human walked hand in tentacle across a laboratory floor.

Ahh noises, scattered clapping and laughter. The man with the horn-rimmed glasses guffawed loudly, startling Hannah.

'Albert and Bertram became friendly, tame almost. They recognised their humans, exhibiting welcoming behaviours and anticipation of reward in the form of food. They *seemed* to develop an affection for their attendants, if it isn't too much of an anthropomorphism to call anything an octopus might experience *affection*. However, this only applied to two of the octopuses that Dews worked with. The third octopus, Charles, was different.'

Another YouTube clip, titled, *The Difficult Octopus.*

'This isn't Charles,' Neville said, 'but this is the kind of behaviour he exhibited.'

The difficult octopus thrashed around in the tank, clearly unhappy at his confinement. He squirted water, then ink, at his attendants, broke the lever he was required to press for food, smashed a jar by pounding it rather than unscrewing the lid, then plugged the valves of his tank with his tentacles until it flooded.

More laughter this time, more clapping. Neville had captured their attention. He was good at this, Hannah thought, with a hollow sensation. Somehow, she hadn't expected him to be good.

'Now, see, isn't that interesting?' Neville said. 'Who's getting more approval here? It almost seems as though you prefer the *unfriendly* octopus to the friendly ones!'

Another ripple of laughter.

'You *do*!' Neville exclaimed. 'Well, there's a thing. Could it be that at some level you all identify more with the unfriendly octopus? Why would that be?'

There was a minor disturbance as Karl and Anton entered the theatre. 'No problem,' Neville said, as Karl lifted a hand in apology. Hannah watched them as they made their way towards two seats at the end of a row, then returned her attention to Neville.

'—fearsome predator,' Neville was saying. 'He was fast, and lethal. He had to be kept in a tank on his own because he would automatically attack other octopuses. He was not *necessarily* better equipped to survive than the other two, who were more conciliatory to their human captors. But he was better equipped to survive in the wild. One might say, in fact, that he was maladapted to the new environment of security, resistant to taming. He remained a predatory beast.

'In human terms we might say he was anti-social, recidivist. Which is, of course, how we describe certain human criminals such as psychopaths. Obviously, we wouldn't describe an octopus that way. But why wouldn't we?'

'Of course,' he continued, when no one answered, 'most comparisons between humans and other animals are spurious – the product of our androcentric view of the world. In the case of octopuses, for example, we know they evolved along a different evolutionary line from us. Humans and octopuses are very distant relatives indeed. In order to look for a common ancestor, you have to go back more than 600 million years. To what is now known as the Ediacaran period.'

An image of a fossil appeared on the screen.

'An Ediacaran life form – named after the region in which it was discovered. It is evidence of animal life that pre-dates the Cambrian era, when animal life was thought to have begun. Since the first finding, in 1946, many other such fossils have been found, and called – wouldn't you know it – Ediacarans.'

Neville scrolled through several similar images. They all looked like oval indentations in rock. Hannah glanced at the clock. Thirty-six minutes to go. Unless there were questions.

There were always questions.

'—rudimentary nervous system but no sense organs, no eyes, no antenna. No pincers, teeth, sensors, stinging or squirting mechanisms. No evidence, therefore, to suggest that Ediacarans interacted with one another by competing for food or mates. They filtered nutrients from the water and had no need to prey on other life forms. It seems likely from the evidence that the Ediacaran world was a peaceful one – one palaeontologist went so far as to call it *The Garden of Ediacaran.*

'Yet from these peaceful, rudimentary beings evolved both human and octopus. Two species manifestly capable of aggression and destruction.'

Towards the front of the room someone started coughing. It turned into a protracted bout. 'Oh *dear*,' Neville said. 'does anyone have any water?'

François leapt forward with a bottle, and Neville waited to resume.

'From the Cambrian period the fossil record contains evidence of eyes, antennae, claws, not found in the Ediacaran. What this means is that animals had started to interact, mainly to prey on one another. This interaction, this predation, triggered evolution. The animals that were most responsive, most alert, had a definite evolutionary advantage. It became necessary to pay attention in order to avoid being eaten.

'I mentioned before, if you remember, the importance of eating. Where would we be without it?'

Laughter.

'We might all still be under a rock, sifting algae. With predation, we became interactive. With predation came evolution. The Ediacaran, living peacefully, minding its own business, was on its way out.

'Animals went from filtering micro-organisms to feeding on dead animals, to hunting living animals. You know the scenes we all turn away from in wildlife documentaries? Lions closing in on a zebra, a spider ingesting a fly. Not the pretty bits. But crucial to evolution.

'Now, the octopus is one of the most fearsome predators of the sea. They have large and complex brains. But they are not like our brains, and they are not like the brains of the group of animals we normally think of as intelligent - chimpanzees, dogs. Those animals are, in certain respects, *like us*. We have a shared history, a shared evolutionary line. We do not have a shared history, not really, with the octopus. Cephalopod intelligence is different from ours in at least one important respect. It is non-social. Or at least, not *very* social.'

Just for a moment, Hannah was distracted by a memory of hiding behind the curtains in a classroom. She'd stayed there the entire lesson, because she didn't like the teacher. No one had noticed she was there.

When she looked back at the screen, a timeline of human evolution had appeared.

'We can see that for the first few million years or so, humanity's main innovation was the use of stone tools. Much later, we have fire. Early human society remains unchanged throughout this time – small, scattered groups of hunter-gatherers, who rarely interacted.'

'Maybe half a million years ago, some kind of speech developed, a proto language that became more complex as larger groups formed. Roughly 200,000 years ago, homo sapiens emerged and superseded other groups, such as Neanderthals. Also, at this time, we have the first evidence of trade. Fifty thousand years ago we have ritual burials – so, some kind of belief system. At a similar time, cave art appears. Maybe twelve thousand years ago we have the first evidence of agriculture, and settlement. After this, we have metalwork and the wheel, then writing. And from *this point on*, it becomes virtually impossible to track the number of human inventions. Try, if you will, to list the number of things that have been invented even in the past year.'

No one tried. Neville looked round slowly and Hannah felt the same compunction again, to hide. *Curtains*. She could see them vividly, as though she was still in the classroom. They were plain and dark, but with vertical lines running through the weave.

That was the kind of child she'd been. A child who wanted to hide things, including herself.

Have you seen my brooch? Her mother's voice said.

Of course she had.

'—advances in technology do not necessarily equal advances in human evolution, but we can certainly see that, as humans come together, in larger groups, technological progress grows exponentially. And why? Because human development is social. We interact, we communicate, we share. Arguably, without these traits, we would have met the same fate as the Ediacarans. We are not faster or stronger than other animals. Our senses are, in many ways, quite limited. What we had was an ability to cooperate and compete, to pool resources and ideas, and develop rules.'

The lecture theatre was absolutely quiet, apart from another brief cough. Hannah felt the urge to check her key again, but told herself to stop. Stop fidgeting. Relax. The discomfort had spread from her hips along her spine to her neck, over her skull. She stretched her neck to one side then another.

'— these rules deviate wildly, from one society and one era to another, but they are always there especially when it comes to sexual behaviour. It's as if we can't allow the sexual instinct to just express itself – what would that lead to? Chaos? The end of the species? Just as we learned to exert some control over reproduction in agriculture, so we exerted many, many controls over human sexual behaviour. To the point where we hardly know what human sexuality is naturally like – are we monogamous or polygamous? Hetero or homosexual? Would we *naturally* have an incest taboo?'

The picture of Adam and Eve came back on the screen.

'No one knows, for certain, how old this story is. Some people will tell you that the Adam and Eve story is five or six thousand years old. If that is so, it would coincide with developments in settled communities and agriculture. Part of Adam's punishment, you may recall, was that food would not be readily available to him any more, he would have to work the land. Some say it refers to law making, the first rules of early society, in which humanity showed awareness of 'good' and 'evil' and 'shame'. But also, in this same story, Adam was given the power of naming, which may take us all the way back to the origins of language.

'Whichever way you look at it, however, it seems likely, that the story of Adam and Eve is less about the origins of humanity itself, than the origins of human society, with its rules and transgressions, its language, and laws.'

Even when he wasn't looking at her, she could feel his gaze on her skin. It made her want to crawl out of it, like a snake. Slither out of the lecture theatre, leaving it behind.

'—most psychopaths being in Parliament,' Neville said, and there was another wave of laughter, at a joke she'd missed.

'However, the traditional idea of the psychopath is of someone outside society, who has definitely broken the rules—'

An image from *The Silence of the Lambs* appeared onscreen.

'Hannibal Lecter,' the man with the horn-rimmed glasses said, quite loudly, looking at Hannah with raised eyebrows. She looked away.

'—think about how destructive humanity is. We are, hands down, the most destructive species on the planet. We have ploughed up the earth, destroyed forests and the habitats of thousands of creatures who are now extinct.

Images of squid and other creatures entangled in plastic.

'We have altered the climate, slaughtered billions of animals for our own nutrition, or for pleasure, and billions of other humans in the course of war. If you were examining a *species* for psychopathology, you would have to put the whole human race on trial. Yet still we single out certain individuals as psychopaths. Only certain ones though.'

A portrait of Henry VIII appeared on screen.

'This guy here, from English history, may have had as many as 70,000 people executed in the course of altering the succession. He had one unfortunate cook boiled alive in his court, while everyone dined. It was quite common, incidentally, for traitors to be hung drawn and quartered in front of the court while they ate.

'We don't call Henry VIII a psychopath. Those members of the Church who burned witches alive, or pressed them to death with stones, are not considered to be psychopaths.

'Today, all over the world, we have oppressive regimes, too many to mention, who routinely violate what we term *human rights*, employing torture, mass starvation.

'*And*, in the course of science, we have achieved remarkable things, often – even usually, at the expense of other creatures.

An image of Laika, the first dog sent into space, never to return.

'In the case of our own science, the study of the human mind, we have been especially inventive. Can we drive an ape mad, by cutting out part of its hippocampus? Yes we can. Can we sever the spinal cord of rats to work out whether they still feel pain? Sure! Can we re-wire the brains of frogs so that they are unable to catch their food? Yep.'

'Yet we still designate only *certain individuals* as pathological. My guess is, if I showed you images of such people . . .'

Images of Dr Shipman, Hitler, Luis Garavito, Mikhail Popkov, appeared on the screen.

'No one's going *aah* now. You're not laughing or clapping. They're not the same as Charles, the unfriendly octopus, are they? How are they not the same?'

Silence. Not even a cough. Eighteen minutes, Hannah thought. No more, surely? Even with questions? And then lunch . . .

'Well, as I said, human consciousness is primarily social, not like the octopus'. It is almost impossible for us to imagine how a non-social consciousness might experience the world. We measure and define everything by whether we act constructively or destructively towards one another . . .'

Of course, she didn't actually *have* to meet him for lunch. She could say she had a headache, perhaps. Her thoughts wandered to Thibaut, to going home with him, packing her case. Hardly anything to pack, really, she'd left most of it in her suitcase already.

'—but let's remember that, as civilisation marches on, it becomes ever more destructive. It's well-nigh impossible to keep in mind all the damage that we are doing just by being a member of the human species. And not just any member, but a member of the first world, the privileged elite.'

'This paper, ladies and gentlemen, that you have sat through so patiently, proposes that we are a pathological species, exhibiting psychopathic behaviours as a *norm*, rather than as deviance, and that all our assessments of pathology and psychopathology in the individuals we treat should be made in that context.'

It sounded as if he might be drawing to a close. Hannah began, just fractionally, to relax. He wasn't talking about her, he hadn't referred to her at all.

'—first, we need to change the kinds of narratives we ourselves.'

'Jung has already proposed that myths and fairy tales represent a kind of negotiation between our conscious and unconscious minds. But what has happened to the fairy story over the centuries? It has been cleaned up. In the earliest versions of Little Red Riding Hood, for example, the girl eats her own grandmother, then takes off her clothes and gets into bed with the wolf.

'That is not the version we tell our children! There are versions of Cinderella in which the ugly sisters cut off their own toes in order to fit them into the glass slipper – an early version of Chinese foot binding, perhaps, since the story seems to have originated in China. We don't hear about the queen wanting to eat the lungs and liver of her stepdaughter in the original version of Snow White.

'What has happened to these stories? We've altered them, to make them more acceptable. In much the same way as we attempt to "clean up" our own historical record – removing from it those elements we find unacceptable. And similarly, we "clean up" the stories we tell about ourselves. Not just for the benefit of other people. We select what we want to remember about ourselves. But we all know that the aspects of ourselves we don't acknowledge tend to erupt in fantasies or dreams.

Joanna and her mother, sitting on the settee.

'What is the *real* reason that we laughed at and clapped the unfriendly octopus? Was it not a moment of recognition, that these dark urges exist within ourselves?'

Weeds in her hair. And they had looked at her with identical eyes.

'This recognition is surely healthier than thinking that

certain people, governments, religions are *bad*, while *we*, on the other hand, are enlightened, and good.'

Holding hands. Apart from the settee, the room had looked like her old classroom. Joanna's classroom. She'd never felt as though she belonged there. All those rooms in her childhood, where she'd never felt as though she'd belonged; at school, even at home.

'—many of you here are lovely people. You donate to good causes, help your neighbour, recycle what you can. Just by doing the job you do, you are helping the human race. That is probably part of your narrative about yourself. A narrative that overlooks that fact that your very existence depends on slaughter, slavery, exploitation and the destruction of the world's resources.'

Only in the Wild had she felt anything like a sense of belonging, that she could expand into herself, become something other than the obedient Hannah she was at school.

'—I'm suggesting, therefore, that the problem may lie not with social *deviance* as such, but with the narratives we create about ourselves that clean up or remove the destructive and predatory elements. By deciding that certain individuals are *not like us*, by labelling them monsters and segregating the acceptable from the unacceptable we separate the civilised from the uncivilised, ostensibly to protect us from danger, just as we do with the land we live on . . .'

Here an image appeared on screen of a sign reading DANGER.

'Actually to avoid looking more closely at ourselves . . .'

A NO PUBLIC ACCESS sign appeared. The camera seemed to be following a path.

With the first glimpse of the reservoir, Hannah felt a current of shock running from her stomach to her chest.

DEEP WATER, the sign read. NO SWIMMING.

'To prevent a full awareness of who we are,' Neville said. Very deliberately, he raised his eyes and looked at Hannah. He'd known where she was all the time.

The impulse to get up and leave the room was so powerful, Hannah felt an actual movement in her flesh, in the soles of her feet. But she remained where she was, staring back at Neville.

'This paper suggests that rather than increasing the number of rules, there is an *urgent* need to alter the stories we tell ourselves about who we are,' Neville said. 'Otherwise, we learn nothing.'

Thank you,' he said, looking away finally. 'Any questions?'

Hannah stood, clutching her bag. Fortunately, her route to the exit was clear.

As she left the theatre she could see the signs in her peripheral vision, posted like white vigilantes on the screen.

DANGER

NO PUBLIC ACCESS

NO SWIMMING

And even in her agitated state, as she hurried towards the lift she thought, *Jo would have liked that.*

XV

HANNAH PACED UP and down, although her room was barely big enough for pacing. When she knocked into the set of drawers she stopped and sat down on the bed.

Breathe.

She closed her eyes, and saw again those white signs in the Wild.

There had been no signs at all in Hannah's childhood. Neville must have made a special trip to take the photos. Before or after leaving the country.

She had a sudden image of firing a gun at him, the explosion of colour on his chest as he collapsed over the lectern.

There was a bitter taste in her mouth. She remembered the smell of rust in the soil, how her hands had tasted of hot copper from the pennies she'd dug into the earth. She remembered the pungent smell of the grass, the sweetish, sickly smell of the water.

She hadn't been to the Wild since *it* happened, yet her brain could re-create the exact memory of its scents.

Hannah pressed the tips of her fingers to her forehead, to the points that relieved tension.

What game was he playing?

Blackmail. It could only be that. But what did he want, and what exactly could he threaten her with?

What have you done? he'd asked.

What did he *think* she'd done?

There was only one way to find out. But she didn't want to talk to him. She wanted to go home.

Hannah rubbed her fingertips across her forehead, forward and back, forward and back.

It isn't fair! Somewhere inside her, that child's cry. It was definitely not fair.

She'd tried so hard. All on her own she'd overcome her problems, her fear of water, her reluctance or inability to speak, her obsessive need to rearrange her room. Even at that age, she'd never, for one moment, relaxed her vigil on herself.

Surely she deserved some credit for that?

She remembered one boy, Joseph, who'd survived a car crash in which his father and brother had died. Four years later he still couldn't sleep, and when he did, he dreamed about the crash, waking drenched in sweat. The moment when his father's car had swerved and hit a wall replayed itself constantly in his mind. When she was talking to him he would judder suddenly at the impact. It was as though his life had also ended at that point.

But Hannah's life hadn't ended. Even though she'd been suddenly and absolutely alienated from the rest of her world. Rumours had spread invisibly, like a virus, or plague; no one knew who was spreading them. There was Joanna's mother, of course, who, in the months that followed *the incident*, became ever more spiky, deranged. She'd attacked a woman in the supermarket once when their trolleys bumped, she smelled of drink.

Hannah's mother grew stiffer, more resolved, pale eyes glittering, lips pressed, spine very straight as though braced for attack. In public she defended Hannah, as though she were the victim; in private, apart from insisting she ate, she hardly spoke to her, and never referred to what had happened.

It was though a screen had come down between them.

But her mother had barely spoken to her anyway. And the other children hadn't played with her, apart from Jo.

The image of Joanna's face rising from the water, mouth open, sinking again, returned to her, but she suppressed it fiercely.

She'd passed unobtrusively through grammar school, then university, making no friends, not even boyfriends. Although once or twice, almost dutifully, she'd slept with other students who'd shown an interest. It meant nothing to her, she'd never thought about them afterwards.

She'd not *had a relationship* with them, or anyone. Until Thibaut.

Thibaut.

He would call her again, just to see if she'd spoken to Neville. She could almost hear herself saying, *yes, of course, it was fine*.

Hannah glanced at her watch. Neville would have finished answering questions by now.

He would be on his way to the Bistro. Perhaps he was already there. Thibaut was expecting her to talk to him.

Did she even want to know why he'd flown half way across the world to speak to her?

No, in fact, she didn't. She wished his plane had crashed on the way.

But it hadn't. He was here, now.

He would have seen her leave the lecture. Possibly, he expected her not to meet him, to spend the rest of the conference hiding.

She felt a twist of rage, like a dark knot in her stomach.

Perhaps she should surprise him by turning up.

XVI

A T THE TOP of the stairs there was a small landing and glass doors that opened onto the roof garden. Hannah could see tables and chairs, and trellises creating alcoves for the tables. All around the perimeter of the garden there was a barrier made from panes of glass, offering an unobstructed view over the lake. That was where most of the tables were.

She wouldn't want to sit there.

Behind her, the lift doors opened. Hannah felt a small shrinking sensation. She turned slowly. Two people walked past her, and there, following them, was Neville.

He stopped when he saw her, she could see him mentally recalibrating.

'Hannah,' he said, and smiled, fractionally later.

'You seem surprised.'

'Not at all – I'm glad you came.' There was a brief pause, then he walked towards the door, and as it glided open, he stood to one side to let Hannah through.

Always the gentleman, her mother said.

They waited together in an uncomfortable, prickling silence until a waiter approached and led them towards the glass fence.

Hannah's mouth felt suddenly dry. Should she ask for a different table? There was hardly anyone in the Bistro. But then Neville would be aware of her discomfort.

That was what he wanted, her discomfort. What excuse could she give?

The moment when she could have said something passed. She followed them mutely to the table.

The waiter pulled a seat out for her and, dutifully, she sat. She looked down at the small bowl containing napkins, the placemats. The lake swam and lurched in her peripheral vision.

Breathe.

'Isn't this lovely?' Neville said, moving his chair. It banged into the table leg, upsetting the small bowl, the condiments.

Without looking directly, Hannah could see a silvery spangle on the surface of the lake. There was the Jet d'Eau with the array of buildings behind it, and the mountains, deposited in the water. At the furthest edge, the lake disappeared into sky.

She agreed that it was beautiful.

'I'm so glad you could join me,' Neville said. 'It would be a pity to leave the conference without having at least one meal together.'

Hannah was saved from responding by the waiter, who took their order for drinks. Neville ordered wine, Hannah Perrier water.

'So tell me,' Neville said, unfolding his napkin, 'what did you think of the lecture?'

Hannah looked towards the only other couple she could see. The woman had a peach silk scarf. And there was another man, sitting alone.

Presumably most people had gone out to eat.

'It ran on, I think,' she said.

'It *did*, didn't it? That's a terrible habit of mine. I'm well known for it at work. Getting carried away while the next group of students are waiting to come in. I imagine your own lectures are perfectly timed.'

Hannah smiled as the waiter passed her a menu. She

studied it carefully. *Soupe à l'oignon, Salade Végétarienne.* Despite missing breakfast, she wasn't hungry at all. And the onion soup would probably come with a layer of cheese.

A different waiter came with a basket of bread and some olives. 'I believe the Puy lentils are very good,' Neville said, leaning towards Hannah confidentially. 'Would you like to share a salad?'

Ratatouille, Hannah thought. The go-to dish for vegans. She put the menu down, looked consideringly at Neville, at the slight sheen of sweat on his forehead, although it wasn't overly warm. His eyes darted around before settling on hers. *Like flies*, she thought. It occurred to her that he was nervous, whereas, now she was here, she felt unexpectedly calm. She studied the menu again.

'But did you *enjoy* it?' he asked.

'I'm sorry?'

'The lecture?'

'Was I meant to enjoy it?'

'I'd rather hoped you would.'

The image of the white signs reappeared in Hannah's mind. 'It was interesting,' she said.

'I'm glad you thought so.'

'If a little - angled.'

'Oh?'

'Conjectural.'

'You think so?'

'More of an opinion piece, perhaps, than a research paper.'

Neville sat back, scraping his chair. 'Well, I guess that's what I thought we were meant to do - think outside the frame, to use Jopi's phrase.'

'Of course,' Hannah said. 'I just think you painted a rather . . . damning picture of the human race.'

'Really?' Neville said. 'In what way?'

'You seem to have a poor opinion of people.'

'Don't you?'

Hannah considered. 'No,' she said, thoughtfully. 'I don't think I do.'

'Well! That's good to hear . . .'

'People can surprise you,' she said, thinking of Michael's father, visiting him so regularly, and of Danny Millfield, who had unexpectedly taken to protecting Martin Hawkes. But she didn't want to think about Danny. Not now. She thought instead about Thibaut.

'They certainly *can*, Neville said, 'Although, not necessarily in a good way.'

The waiter interrupted them again. Hannah ordered the ratatouille, Neville the lentil ragout. 'Salad?' he queried, raising his eyebrows at her and she said '*Sans fromage, sans oeufs*,' to the waiter.

'Oh – are you vegan? In Switzerland? That must be tough.'

'You get used to it,' she said.

'And more bread,' Neville said to the waiter. 'I've tried being vegan,' he added, as the waiter left, 'but it never lasts long. I guess I'm just too fond of cheese.'

Hannah looked deliberately, casually, over the lake. A steamer passed slowly across her line of vision, disappearing behind the Jet d'Eau. She remembered the sign saying, DEEP WATER.

'Where did you get those images from,' she asked, 'at the end?'

'Yes,' Neville said, dipping his bread in the oil. 'I thought you might recognise them.' He chewed, for a while, then said, 'I went back. Just to see what had changed – if anything. As it turned out, quite a lot had. New houses, a roundabout at one end of the street, traffic bumps. And all those signs! But the Wild itself is still there - and the reservoir, of course.'

Hannah picked up a roll, broke it in two, considered her next question carefully. 'Was it strange, going back?' she asked.

'It *was!*' Neville said, his mouth full. 'Like looking at two places at once, the one in your memory, and the one as it is now. Extraordinary!'

Hannah said nothing. Images of the Wild passed rapidly through her mind.

'I walked all the way around it,' Neville continued, helping himself to another roll, 'before going down to the reservoir itself. And you know what struck me most?'

Hannah shook her head.

'How small it was! Took me less than half an hour to walk all the way round. And when we were children, it seemed *huge!*'

It had seemed infinite to Hannah, like a separate world with its own dimensions. Time and space were different there. She remembered the tracks, leading nowhere, the stumps of trees covered in ivy, sprouting fern. How easy it was, if you fell behind, to lose sight of the person you were with, to become utterly lost. She shook her head again.

'I *know,*' Neville said. '*the past is a different country.*' He smiled at her and a large crumb of crust fell from his mouth to the table. Hannah looked away.

The drinks arrived, another basket of bread, and a jug of water, then the salad. Hannah unfolded her napkin.

'I wasn't sure what I was going to do with them at first,' Neville said. 'I just hoped, that somehow, I would have the chance to show them to you. Of course - I didn't know whether we'd meet - but now - here you are!'

'I am,' agreed Hannah.

'Here we both are – together!' said Neville, and he raised his glass to her. Hannah tipped her bottle of Perrier in his direction.

'I think you might have had *some* idea that we might meet,' she said.

'I'm sorry?'

'You weren't actually surprised, I think, when we met in the foyer?'

'Oh?'

'Perhaps you'd done your research already?'

Neville smiled modestly, then raised his hands. 'You got me,' he said.

'And you flew all the way from New Zealand just to see me, when the lecture would be available, to anyone who knows Jopi, online. I'm assuming you wouldn't have done that without a reason.'

Neville chewed, nodding slowly.

'So, are you going to tell me what that is?' she asked.

'Oh!' Neville said, as though surprised. 'I thought you might like to catch up first. Have some salad,' he said, passing her the bowl. Hannah took a small scoop.

'Catch up?' she said.

Neville lowered the salad bowl. 'Yes, you know,' he said, 'on everything that's happened since we last met.'

Forty years ago, Hannah thought. As though reading her mind, he said, 'I realise that's some territory to cover. But I do have one or two questions I'd like to ask.'

'Fire away,' Hannah said. But then the rest of the food arrived. The ratatouille was not the way she made it, in a thick stew, it was heaped into a small tower, with layers of roasted aubergine, pepper, courgette, trimmed with herbs. The waiter drizzled it with oil. Neville's ragout came with a circle of grilled goat's cheese on top.

'Oh, that looks *good*,' he said.

'If you like cheese,' said Hannah. She poured more water into her glass. The sense that she was somewhere outside herself, that there were two of her, one acting and one watching, was intensifying. As though the observing part didn't know what the other Hannah might say, or do.

'You know,' Neville said, 'you could have ordered this ragout without the cheese – it's delicious!'

'I'm fine.'

'I'm so glad we've got this time together, without the group, you know?'

'Sure.'

'Because – and really, I don't want this to take up too much time – but I did want to fill in some of the gaps – tell you something about my own story, first – if that's OK with you?'

Hannah opened her hands, then pressed them together again. 'I'm listening,' she said.

XVII

'YOU KNOW, OF course, where my house was – where I grew up?'

Hannah did know. Neville had lived on the other side of The Wild, in one of the 50 or 60 new houses that had been built despite public opposition. Campaigners said they didn't want to lose any of the green areas in the town, and there were perfectly good old terraces that could have been renovated. But the local property developer had some influence with the council and in an improbably short time, a portion of the Wild had disappeared and a number of identical, box-like houses, built in cul-de-sacs, with open lawns, had taken its place.

'Backhanders,' Hannah's mother had said, although she had no interest in the Wild, except as a place of Danger, and they could only see the tops of the new houses in winter, when the trees were bare.

Neville's parents had been among the first to move in, so Neville had gone to the same primary school as Hannah. And like Hannah, he was an only child.

'My mother had five or six miscarriages – did you know that?'

Hannah didn't – why would she? 'That's sad,' she murmured.

'Isn't it? Five or six miscarriages – and then me. Their much-wanted, only son. Wanted by my mother anyway – I think I was always a bit of a disappointment to my dad.' He dabbed at his mouth with his napkin. 'But you remember what kind of child I was, right?'

Hannah made a non-committal noise. She began deconstructing the tower of ratatouille one segment at a time, looking with disfavour at the oily sauce.

'Not very sporty, bit of a geek – never fitted in. The other boys would *kick my ass* if I tried to join them.' He grinned broadly at the Americanism, and Hannah saw a strand of lettuce clinging to the gap between his front teeth. 'Rubbed my face in the dirt, threw my trainers in the pond – one time they shut me in a garage and I was locked up in there all day!' He raised his eyebrows, shook his head, chuckled ruefully. 'Even I learned my lesson after that. I used to hide from them. And of course, one of the best places to hide was on the Wild. That's how I knew you and Joanna played there. I used to follow you a little – at a distance – I didn't want to disturb you.'

That wasn't how Hannah's mother had seen it. '*Spying* on you, the little creep.' she'd said. 'He's probably hoping to *see something he shouldn't!*'

Hannah knew exactly what she meant but she couldn't help herself, she'd said, 'Such as?' and the broken veins on her mother's cheeks had darkened. She rarely made any reference to sex without making it sound like atrocity not to be countenanced or borne.

'You know what I mean,' she'd hissed. 'If you must go to that place – just keep yourself decent – don't *take anything off!*'

Hannah remembered lowering her eyes, wanting to laugh. They didn't *take anything off*, in any case, apart from their shoes and socks. And sometimes they tucked their skirts into their knickers.

'They made so much of that, at the time, if you remember,' Neville said, 'the fact that I used to hang around the two of you. But really, it was all quite innocent! I just used to like – seeing you together, I suppose. You seemed so different, away from school – so *free*.'

That was how she'd felt, Hannah remembered. Free. She looked down at her plate, to disguise a sudden emotion, dabbed at the oil with a crust of bread.

'Well, they would keep coming back to that, wouldn't they?' Neville said. 'Given the circumstances. Her parents would have wanted to know whether she'd been – *interfered with*, was the popular phrase at the time, I believe. More bread?'

He waved the basket towards her. Hannah shook her head. 'I don't see where all this is getting us,' she said. 'I *know* what happened.'

'Do you?' he said, lowering the basket. 'Do you know how many times I was questioned?'

'I was questioned too!' Hannah said. It had seemed to go on for months, although it was probably only weeks. Her memory of that summer was distorted; there was only *before*, and *after*, as though the time between was an island, separate from the rest of her life.

'I know,' Neville said. 'And it must have been terrible. I guess, like me, you just wanted it to stop. Is that why you told them I'd done it?'

Hannah stared at him. She could feel heat creeping up her neck into her face.

'What?' she whispered.

'That's why they kept coming back to me,' Neville said. 'Because of what you said.'

She shook her head, as though to shake the memory out of it. 'I – no! That's not—'

'They told me you did. When I protested my innocence – they said, *that's not what the little girl says.*'

Hannah put down her knife and fork. 'If that's what they told you, they were twisting my words.'

'Really?' said Neville. 'Only they read me your testimony from a notebook – I remember that vividly. *Neville was there. He did it.*'

Hannah shook her head violently. 'No!' she said. 'That's not what I said.'

Neville put his own knife and fork down. 'Why don't you tell me what you did say?'

Hannah shook her head again more slowly this time, looking down. She could hear her mother's voice sharply in her mind. *Why don't you leave the child alone – she's already answered you a hundred times! Why aren't you questioning that little lad – the creepy one? He was always following them around – watching – why don't you ask him what he was doing?*

We will, of course, the policewoman had said, but her mother wouldn't stop.

He's not right in the head, that one, if you ask me – always lurking around, spying on them – up to no good! If anyone did anything to that poor girl it'd be him!

The police woman had looked at Hannah. *Is that right, Hannah?* she'd said, gently. *Did Neville do something to Joanna?*

But by that time, Hannah had retreated into silence. Selective mutism, they called it. *Aphasia voluntaria.* Either because she was not in the habit, ever, of contradicting her mother, or because she just wanted it all to go away.

Of course he did! Her mother said. *You can tell just by looking at her that she saw him! She's too shocked and upset to speak!*

And the police woman had leaned forward. *Did you see him, Hannah?*

The memories passed through Hannah's mind so swiftly, in less time than it took to roll the edge of her napkin between her finger and thumb.

Once her mother had said that, about Neville, the questions had stopped for a while. Eventually they'd been notified of the outcome of the investigation.

Hannah looked up. 'You weren't accused of anything,' she said. 'The verdict was accidental death . . .'

Neville smiled. 'That's right, it was,' he said. 'But it didn't end there, did it? For either of us?'

Then he said, 'Do you know what school I went to, after Rosehill?'

Hannah was disconcerted by this apparent change of direction. 'You – didn't you pass the eleven plus?'

'I did,' Neville agreed. 'I even started at the local grammar school. But everyone there *knew*, Hannah – the kids, the teachers. I was the boy who might have done terrible things to a little girl – and then drowned her. Even though I was never charged. Mud sticks, Hannah – we both know that. Isn't that what this conference is all about – give a kid a bad name, and so on?'

Hannah said nothing. *Mud*, she was thinking. Mud on her clothes, her hands and knees, as she'd scrambled up that bank.

'I didn't deal with it too well,' Neville went on. 'I became what you or I might call a *child exhibiting difficult or problematic behaviours*. Locking myself away – wetting the bed, stealing things. And then, at around the same time, my mother became ill. It took a while for them to diagnose it, but eventually – well, they said it was multiple sclerosis. You know, where the nervous system fails to send the right messages to the brain? In the end, she couldn't swallow, or breathe.'

'I'm sorry,' Hannah said, inadequately. 'I didn't know.'

'Why would you? By that time you were at university. Pursuing your career. I don't suppose you gave me a second thought, did you?'

Hannah looked down. That wasn't true. But she'd always tried not to think about him. Until he'd appeared at this conference.

'Anyway, if you remember, my father didn't want much to do with me. Especially after what happened. I was always under the impression that he never quite believed in my innocence. My mother did, bless her, but by that time she wasn't coping too well. And my father couldn't cope with either of us, not really. So he sent me away, to a special school for children with behavioural problems – Grange Moor – perhaps you know it?'

Hannah had heard of it.

'A boarding school – not quite Borstal.' Neville managed an unconvincing smile. 'I was bullied, of course, remorselessly. Who knows – Borstal might have been better? You know I didn't pass a single exam?'

Speechlessly, Hannah shook her head.

'I was past forty when I finally qualified as a therapist. And *then* I couldn't get a job. In the end, I had to get a bit creative with my cv. And I managed to get a paper published – through a friend of a friend – which landed me my first *real* job – at Nottingham. Then a book contract and now – here I am.'

He spread his hands, but he wasn't smiling now. 'By that time, my mother had died – I wasn't there when it happened – my father didn't think to send for me. I'd started college, but I just walked out. Never returned. Took to loading shelves, in a supermarket.'

Hannah made herself look at him. His eyes were wet and brown. Retreating behind his glasses, like snails into their shells.

You could tell the magnitude of what had happened to him in his eyes.

She blinked and looked away. 'I don't know what to say,' she said. 'It must have been . . .' *terrible for you*, she didn't say. *Unimaginable*. She swallowed her words in a breath.

There was a heavy, impenetrable pause. A question was pressing from the back of Hannah's mind, but she wasn't sure she could ask it. It might sound inappropriate, or callous. After a moment, however, she raised her head slowly and said, 'So, how did you find me?'

'What?'

'It's not as though I publicise my work.'

'You don't, do you?' Neville agreed. He wiped his lips again. 'I must admit, I tried one or two avenues that led nowhere. *Friends Reunited*, that kind of thing. Only, *surprise!* No one wanted to be my friend. Yours either, I should imagine.'

Hannah didn't smile.

'I even considered contacting your mother - I suspected she hadn't moved. But I also suspected she'd give me short shrift if I did. Not one to mince words, your mother—'

This did make Hannah smile, wryly.

'—and I don't think I was ever her favourite person, really, was I? So I investigated social media - Facebook, LinkedIn - nothing. You really do keep a low profile, don't you?'

Hannah inclined her head.

'In the end it was that same friend who helped me get published. He lent me one of your articles. About subjectivity. Which I read with great interest, as you can imagine. Although I didn't realise it was you, until I saw your photo in a medical journal.'

Hannah knew which one he meant. They'd asked for a photograph and she hadn't submitted one, so they'd somehow got hold of the small, passport sized one she had to use for her ID.

'I still wasn't sure – it wasn't very clear. And you'd changed your name by then.'

It was true – she'd only really started to publish once she was Hannah Rossier.

'But I thought, Hannah/Annie – was it possible? And the journal gave the details of what else you'd written and I followed it all up, everything! Wonderful work, really remarkable. You might say you helped me to find my own path!'

Hannah smiled, incredulously. 'You didn't go into psychotherapy because of me?'

'Oh, no – not entirely. I got interested in it because of my own experience – as I suspect you did. You know people always think therapists are such empathetic people – but in my experience, the reverse is true – I mean, look at Freud!'

Hannah said nothing.

'No – the vast majority of us are in it to sort out our own shit. But reading your work definitely helped to clarify my areas of interest. You might say I'm your biggest fan-boy!'

He beamed at her. The strand of lettuce was still there, now augmented by a clump of lentils. Hannah had to look away.

'The journals led me to your place of work,' he said, 'So now, here we both are.'

'Yes,' Hannah said, 'and you still haven't told me what you really want to say.'

Neville scraped his chair again and his knee hit the table leg. 'Haven't I? I'd've thought it was obvious.'

'Not really.'

'Seriously?'

'If you want me to apologise, for saying something I can't even remember, then I will. I'm really sorry if anything I said as a child hurt you or made your life difficult in any way.'

'Well, that's good to hear,' Neville said, chewing once more. 'But, obviously, not enough.'

'Why don't you tell me what might be enough? Ever since we met I feel as though you've been trying to say something. It might be clear to you, but it isn't to me. What is it that you'd really like to say?'

For the first time since she'd met him, Neville looked angry. His face congested, she could see the tendons in his neck. He leaned forward, there was a blast of garlic on his breath.

'Don't give me that therapist-speak. I know this shit, remember?'

Hannah gazed at him steadily.

'I'm *saying* that you accused me of something, all those years ago, that I hadn't done. And you *knew* I hadn't done it. All those times I was questioned, I kept thinking, *Annie knows I didn't do it – she'll speak up soon* – even when I was in that shithole of a boarding school, I kept on somehow, ridiculously, thinking you'd say something to someone – clear my name – but you never did. Took me years to realise you never would.'

He sat back again, bumping the table once more.

Hannah managed to keep the surprise from her face. *Was that it?* she thought. *Was that really all he was accusing her of?* She said, 'But you were cleared.'

'What?'

'The investigation was dropped – there was a verdict of accidental death. No one thought you'd . . .'

Killed her, she thought, but she couldn't say that.

'Done anything,' she finished, lamely.

'No one?' Neville said. 'Apart from my parents, of course. And the police officers. And the whole community. Do you know what it's like to be condemned by public opinion? No. Because it didn't happen to you. It happened to me. Because no one knew the truth, apart from you. And you weren't saying, were you?'

He had raised his voice. The woman with the peach-coloured scarf was glancing towards them. Hannah looked at the crumpled surface of the lake. Then she looked back at Neville.

'How dare you?' she said, quietly.

'What?'

'How dare you suggest I didn't suffer from public opinion? I stayed in my room for the next seven years, virtually – I barely left until I went to university. I had no friends, we went nowhere, my mother and I, we couldn't go out without people whispering and pointing. Because everyone thought, just like you, that it wasn't an accident.'

'What do you mean, just like me?'

'I bumped into you – at the top of the bank. And you asked me what I'd done. Those were your exact words – *what have you done?*'

From the look of absolute blankness on Neville's face, Hannah realised that he had no memory of saying those words.

He shook his head, his face utterly baffled. 'I said – what?'

'You said, *What have you done?* to me. I remember it clearly.'

'Well, I don't remember it – and I certainly don't think—' He paused. Hannah could see him casting his mind back, reeling the memories in. 'I remember you looked as though you'd hurt yourself – your hands and knees were bleeding. I might have said something about that.'

Hannah looked away. She could feel a great pressure behind her eyes. She hardly ever cried.

Not for her best friend, certainly not for her mother. Not during all those years of loneliness, when she'd seemed as remote and cut off from the world as some distant satellite that could orbit but never land.

She blinked two or three times.

'So you weren't—' she said. 'You didn't—?'

'Are we talking about you now?' Neville said. 'Because I actually thought this conversation was about me.'

Hannah shook her head. 'I don't know what you want from me,' she said.

'Really? Weren't you in the lecture? Didn't you hear me talking about the importance of changing the narrative?'

Hannah shook her head again in incomprehension.

'You know – changing the record – saying what really happened . . .'

'Who to? The police? Isn't it a bit late for that? Considering the investigation closed forty years ago—'

'No, no,' Neville interrupted her. 'I mean here, at this conference. Now.'

Hannah looked at him incredulously, then laughed.

'In your lecture, I mean. Don't you see? We're here, at a conference about criminal psychology – it's the perfect place to talk about what happened.'

So he didn't want to expose her, he wanted Hannah to do that job for him. She laughed again.

'We're talking about innocence and guilt and the whole spectrum of things that lie between – things we don't even have a name for – partial, or unwitting guilt. Partial innocence – is that a thing? *Should* it be a thing?'

When Hannah still didn't speak, he went on, 'We're

looking at the many, many ways in which the system ca[n]
the child – all the loopholes – all the prejudices, all th[e]
in which a child can be lost. I mean – look at you and me,
for instance – who was the plausible one – who was believed?
And who was accused?

'If we can't talk about these things at a conference like this,'
he continued, 'then where can we? And these things should be
talked about – they should be opened up to discussion. And
I think it would do you good.'

'Do me good?' Hannah repeated.

'I'm giving you a chance to let the trapdoor open, Hannah
– the trapdoor you've kept locked all these years. With little
Annie on the other side.'

Hannah was speechless for a moment, at this image of
herself. Then she said, 'You're *mad.*'

'Is that a technical term, professor?' Neville asked. 'What's
the problem here? Your reputation? I lost mine years ago, but
I got it back. You might even find it *enhances* your reputation
– after all, who is more qualified to talk about the criminal
child than you? And if it's *shame* – well then – surely the only
way to deal with that is to bring it out into the open? Shame
is a problem in itself, Hannah – that's what I was trying to
say in my lecture.'

'Have you finished?' Hannah said.

'No, not quite.'

'What you're suggesting is ridiculous – for two reasons.
Firstly, you're saying I accused you of something you didn't
do, and because of that, your life fell apart. But that's wrong.
I didn't accuse you of anything other than being there, which
you were.'

'That's not—' Neville began, but Hannah swept on: *'That's
why the police had to ask you all those questions. If your*

parents didn't believe in your innocence – that's quite a different issue, wouldn't you say? Secondly – I don't see how I can be blamed for your mother's illness – or your father's response to it.'

'MS can lie dormant for years,' Neville said. 'It's often triggered by a shock, or trauma.'

'Even so,' said Hannah, after a breath. 'If you apply just a bit of logic to that situation, I think you'll see I wasn't to blame. I was a *child*, for God's sake, and I'd just seen my best friend drown. I hardly knew what I was saying. And in the end, if you remember, I stopped talking altogether.'

'Great tactic,' Neville said.

'It wasn't a *tactic*,' said Hannah. 'I was traumatised – just as you were – probably even more so. And hardly responsible for the attitudes and prejudices of adults. I'm sorry for what happened to you – my life wasn't exactly a party either! But people haven't come here – to an academic conference – to watch it being turned into some kind of talk show – or – vendetta! It certainly isn't what Jopi wants!'

Neville nodded, slowly. His arms were folded across his chest. Hannah couldn't read his expression. 'Very well,' he said. 'But I'm offering you a chance, here.'

'What chance?'

'The chance to *change the record*. You won't take it, because you don't want to be exposed. Which means that shame wins.'

'What *shame*?'

'Haven't you spent your life hiding, Hannah?'

For a moment, she didn't speak. Then she said, 'You haven't the faintest idea what my life has been like.'

'No?' said Neville. 'Why don't you tell me?'

Several images raced through Hannah's mind: the flashing lights, her mother's face, all the questions. Years of isolation, anxiety, depression, OCD. All those years when she'd never, even for a moment, stopped being afraid.

She shook her head. 'I can't,' she said. It wasn't what she'd meant to say, but it was true.

Neville stood up, towering over her. Then he turned towards the view. 'Such a pretty country,' he said. 'I can see why you like it here. Hard to see beyond all that beauty. Like a mask, really, hiding all kinds of things beneath.'

He leaned over the glass fence.

Some years earlier, Hannah had studied aikido. She'd learned how to shift the balance of opponents much bigger than her. She could imagine toppling Neville over the side of the fence, into the lake. No one was watching. She could almost hear the splash.

He turned around. 'So you're not going to take my offer?' he asked.

Hannah sighed. Injecting weariness into her voice she said, 'If you mean, am I going to stand up before all the delegates here and recount the story of something that happened forty years ago rather than giving my prepared lecture, then no, I'm not going to do that. It would be inappropriate and a total waste of time.'

Neville nodded. 'OK,' he said.

'OK?'

'I've given you a chance,' he said. 'Which was more than you gave me. if you won't take it, that's up to you.'

His shadow moved over her. 'Are you threatening me?' she said.

'I'm just trying to open up the discussion.'

To make me confess, she wanted to say. But she wouldn't give him that satisfaction. She could sense him looking at her. His gaze was like a touch, crawling over her skin.

She could always say he'd tripped. But with her luck, Neville would probably be rescued.

'Anton had to leave, you know,' he said. 'Did you know his partner has dementia?'

At the look of confusion on her face, he said, 'He's a lot older than Anton, I believe – but still, it's a tough deal. And we'll miss out on his paper, which was about Alzheimer's. But I've already asked Jopi if I can step in for him. So I'll be giving the lecture just before yours.'

Hannah nodded to herself. That was it, then. That was what he would do.

'Two lectures in two days?' she said. 'People might feel overwhelmed.'

'Oh, I hope I can keep them entertained,' he said, blandly.

With sudden decision, Hannah screwed up her napkin, picked up her bag. 'How much do I owe you?' she asked.

'Oh, no, please,' Neville said. 'This one's on me,' He smiled. 'It'll go on my account.'

She squinted up at him for a moment, then thought *what the hell*, and stood up, dusting her trousers. 'Good luck with your lecture,' she said. 'I hope it achieves whatever it is you want it to achieve.'

'Hannah,' said Neville, but she was already walking away. She smiled at the man sitting on his own, the woman in the peach-coloured scarf, both of whom were looking their way.

'I'll see you tomorrow, then, at the lecture,' Neville said to her retreating back. 'Looking forward to it!' he called after her.

XVIII

HANNAH IGNORED THE lift, taking the stairs at a pace. Several images were racing through her mind. Joanna's face in the water, scrambling up that bank, bumping into Neville, then running, running to Joanna's house, but no one was in. Or, at least, no one answered the door. Only after Hannah had run round to the front door and banged on that, had Joanna's oldest brother finally opened it. He was half-dressed, with a sleepy, blurred expression on his face. Hannah couldn't make him understand.

Then she'd seen her mother, walking back from the hospital, still in her uniform, and the hat she always wore.

She hadn't cried until then, but when she reached her mother she burst into tears straight away.

Her mother hadn't hugged Hannah, like any normal mother. She'd gripped her shoulders. *What is it?* she'd said. *What have you done?*

But that was Neville, not her mother. What had her mother said?

She couldn't remember.

Hannah let herself into her room, pressed the door shut behind her. She put her bag down, kicked off her shoes and sat on the bed.

Why had she agreed to meet him?

It had achieved nothing, apart from allowing him to threaten her. To show her the full extent of his hostility.

And drag her back into a childhood she'd spent most of her life trying to escape.

I'm giving you a chance to let the trapdoor open, Hannah – the trapdoor you've kept locked all these years. With little Annie on the other side.

It was as though he'd picked a scab from her mind and the memories were flowing freely, in no particular order. She remembered her mother at the reservoir, but not how she got there. Neville was there as well, in the water, pulling at Joanna, her mother had screamed at him to fetch help. Then her mother was in the water, and Joanna – Joanna's face was grey, there were weeds in her hair.

She remembered her mother straddling Joanna, pounding her chest. Her mother's hat had fallen off; Annie could see her scalp where her hair had started to fall out. Eventually she'd sat back, turned her face to the sky.

God be merciful unto me – a sinner! she'd cried.

That was what Hannah remembered, but why would she say that? It made no sense.

She remembered little else, perhaps she'd fainted? Although there was the ambulance, the flashing blue light.

Who was that psychologist who'd suggested that an hour after an event we can only retrieve roughly 50 per cent of information? Ebbinghaus.

And there was Neisser, who'd said that memory was like palaeontology. *Out of a few bone chips, we remember a dinosaur.*

Neville, asking her, *what have you done?*

She'd thought he was accusing her of something terrible, but he'd only meant that it looked as though Hannah had hurt herself.

He couldn't even remember saying it.

With a muffled moan, she lay on the bed.

He was accusing her of lying, of ruining his life. That was what he would tell everyone, in his lecture.

And she would say, what? That she hadn't accused him, it had all been a mistake. Her mother might have said something, but not Hannah. Hannah had just wanted it all to go away. She couldn't remember much beyond that.

But there was a moment she did remember, when she'd looked into the broad, friendly, face of the lady police officer – it was speckled all over like a sparrow's egg, she remembered that. It had an encouraging, confiding expression.

'I just want you to tell us, in your own words,' she'd said.

And Hannah had managed, somehow, to say what she had to say, to shift attention away from her.

But she hadn't accused Neville, that was wrong. A false memory. She let her mind close over it as the surface of water closes over a stone.

MS can lie dormant for years. It's often triggered by a shock, or trauma.

Shit.

Shit.

It would never end, that day by the reservoir. It would never, ever end.

Neville had suffered because of her, so now he wanted her to pay. And there was nothing she could do. Nothing. Other than attend his lecture, to find out what he would say.

She didn't have to attend.

But then she wouldn't know.

What *could* he say? Other than exposing Hannah's past, the past she'd taken such pains to conceal? That would be unpleasant, yes; unbearable, even. But he could only say, surely, that there had been a mistake, not even a miscarriage of justice? He hadn't been charged.

Whatever he said would be damaging, whatever she said would make it worse. Should she deny it, or plead that she'd been a different child then, there? A different person forty years ago? *The past is a different country.*

But the world wasn't interested in forgiveness, in *moving on.* It trapped people like flies on the sticky sheets of history.

She'd worked so hard to build her life, when she could have sunk into a spiral of depression or drug-taking, or crime. All the odds were stacked against traumatised children completing their education, building a career, a home, a marriage. But she, Hannah, had done all that, without state intervention, therapeutic support, without a mother she could turn to or confide in.

None of that would count for anything, after Neville's lecture.

She screwed her eyes up tightly, hugged herself. Thought again of pushing him over that rail, his arms and legs flailing, the look of horror on his face. She could hear the satisfying splash.

But that wasn't real. This was real, this moment now, in which she was trapped.

Unless she disappeared. She'd done it before, and she could do it again. But where would she go?

Curled on the bed, Hannah began to will herself to disappear. It was something she used to do in childhood, to numb the pain. First her feet would disappear, then her ankles, her shins and knees. She could actually feel a sensation of numbness in the soles of her feet. Gradually her mind folded in on itself, becoming blank. She was startled when her phone buzzed, for a moment she couldn't think where it was. Slowly, she sat up, reached for her bag.

Thibaut.

'There you are, *cherie*! *Ça va?*'

'Fine, thank you.'

'*Fine, thank you?*'

She realised how impersonal she sounded. 'Sorry, sorry – it's fine, everything's fine.'

'Well – good.' He paused. 'I was worried about you.'

'I'm fine.'

'Did you see that friend you were telling me about?'

'Mm.'

'And? You said he wanted to talk – about what happened in your childhood?'

'He did, yes.'

'So what did he say?'

'He said – he just has some issues, that's all – painful memories.'

'And what did you say?'

'I – I said what I usually say.'

'Which is?'

Hannah sighed. It was almost unbearable to speak. 'I . . . told him that . . . memory can become a form of self-punishment, of chastisement – that the important thing is to remember it isn't real – to create a distance between yourself and your memories, so you can look at them impersonally, rather than being caught up in them – entangled . . .'

There was a pause.

'Isn't he a therapist himself?'

'I believe so, yes.'

'So surely he would know that?'

I know this shit – remember?

'It's one thing to know it and another to put it into practice.'

'True. So you talked it through?'

139

'A little, yes.'

'And he felt better?'

'I – think so.'

'You think so – you don't know? Will you see him again?'

'I'm not his therapist.'

'Don't do this to me, Hannah,' Thibaut said.

'Do what?'

'Go distant on me – you do it all the time!'

'I'm not.'

'You might as well be on the moon as in Geneva. This is me, remember? Your husband, Thibaut! I know you Hannah, I know when something's not right.'

You don't know me.

'I think I should come to the conference.'

'What? No!'

'Yes – I have a meeting, but I can cancel it – I'll come to you.'

'Thibaut, you mustn't!'

'Why not? I can take you home afterwards. And I can speak to this Neville person if necessary.'

'No!'

'You think I don't know when you're upset? This – Neville – he has upset you, and I don't like it. I won't have it. I will come, and listen to your lecture, and if he has anything to say, he can say it to me!'

Hannah summoned all her strength. 'Thibaut, you are *not* to come here!'

'You don't want me?'

'That's not what I—'

'You want me to stay out of your affairs?'

'Thibaut—'

'I understand.'

You don't!

'You want me to stay away.'

'Thibaut, listen to me – it's not that I don't want you to come – but there's no point! I'm not upset, I'm only tired.'

'Tired?'

'Yes, tired.'

Tired of everything, she didn't say. *Tired of keeping it all together.*

'Well then, if you're tired, you can come home with me today. You don't have to stay for the rest of it.'

'Thibaut, stop. Stop it, now.'

There was a different note in her voice, she could tell he was startled. She softened her tone.

'I know you only want to – look after me – and I appreciate it, I really do. But I'm not walking out on this conference. And I can fight my own battles. Really. How will it look if you step in and start fighting them for me? It will look as though I'm incapable, as though I need defending – when I don't.'

'It's not a question of—'

'I mean it. Thibaut – don't cancel your meeting.'

'But Hannah, I'm worried about you.'

'I know you are, but I've told you – I'm only tired.'

As she said it she realised that she was, in fact, exhausted. She needed to sleep.

'But it's no problem for me – I can be there.'

'Thibaut. You're not listening.'

'I am listening. I'm listening to everything you're not telling me.'

Hannah swallowed. He was such a good, good man.

'I'll tell you everything – after the conference. But I need you to – to have some faith in me,'

'Hannah, you know I do.'

'And leave me to sort things out in my own way. Can you do that?'

She held the silence, willing him to understand. After a long moment, he spoke.

'Very well, Hannah. I will stay away. I will not come to your lecture. But I will come after the conference is over, to bring you home.'

'But—'

'No buts, Hannah. That's what I'm going to do.'

She sighed again. 'Ok, but—'

'Was that a *but*?'

'No. It's fine.'

'Fine.'

'Yes, fine! I'll meet you after the conference.'

'*Bien* - and you can introduce me to Neville.'

'That's not going to happen.'

Thibaut muttered an imprecation in French. 'You are a very stubborn woman.'

'Not stubborn, Thibaut - tired. I'm exhausted. I really need to sleep.'

'So, sleep. I will see you tomorrow.'

'I love you.'

'But not enough to introduce me to your friend?'

'Thibaut!'

'No, no, it's fine. *Tout va bien.* Get some sleep. I love you too.'

The line went dead. Hannah shook her head hopelessly at the phone. Then she lay down on the bed again, curling onto her side. She could feel pressure in her forehead, a sense of pollution swarming up from her stomach and chest, almost as though she'd been poisoned. Or as if she was drowning in foul water.

At least, hopefully, she'd stopped Thibaut from coming until after the conference. She couldn't bear him to hear whatever Neville had to say.

Although, doubtlessly he would hear all about it, soon enough.

And then everything would change.

When she'd first met Thibaut, she hadn't believed in his love for her. Only the weight of his devotion, phoning her every day, or texting her, sending photos to her phone, never, for one moment allowing her to forget he was there, waiting and hoping to see her again, had finally convinced her. That was the first time she'd ever believed she was loved. *Only because he didn't know her,* she'd thought. Now, after eleven years of marriage, she could hardly accuse him of that. Despite the things he didn't know.

The fact that he could love her had made her believe she was worthy of love.

She closed her eyes and saw the image of the Inuit man wandering out into the snow.

How often had she wanted to disappear from her life?

Less often since she'd met Thibaut. It would hurt him too much. He would never get over it. Because he loved her.

She could leave the conference today, or first thing tomorrow, take a train somewhere, anywhere, never return. It would save Thibaut, since whatever came out about her would hurt him as well.

But he loved her. The thought coiled round her like a rope as she drifted into sleep.

XIX

SLEEP CLAIMED HER, inescapably. Her body and mind closed down.

There was a jumble of confused and blurred images. Someone was following her around a large, old building, like an empty factory, but when she opened a door she was in her bedroom in Lucerne. Thibaut was there, although she couldn't see him. It was night time, and she sank onto the bed with him. His arms were around her. With the tips of her fingers, she felt his face, his cheekbones, the promontory of his nose, as she would, sometimes, before making love.

Her fingers became urgent, she wanted him, she was moaning with lust. It took a moment to realise that his beard had gone, he must have shaved it.

Then she knew it wasn't Thibaut. It was Neville.

Hannah started awake, heart pounding. Someone was knocking at the door. *Neville*, she thought, in terror. But Jopi's voice said, 'Hannah, are you there?'

Hannah stumbled off the bed. She would put Jopi off, say she was trying to sleep. 'Jopi,' she said, opening the door.

Jopi was a blaze of colour; orange shirt, floral waistcoat, dazzling palazzo trousers. Hannah blinked at her.

'Are you all right?' Jopi said. 'You look terrible.'

'I was asleep.'

'Oh – I'm so sorry – shall I come back?'

Her face was anxious, kind. Still in the penumbra of sleep,

Hannah said, 'No – not at all,' and stepped back to allow Jopi in. Her mind seemed to be grappling with several problems at once. She moved her bag from the computer chair. 'Please – sit,' she said.

'You're sure? I only came by because I've seen hardly anything of you – and tomorrow is the last day.'

The last day.

Neville's lecture.

She couldn't think about that. 'Tea?' she said, picking up the small kettle.

'Marvellous,' said Jopi. 'Although, I have to say, I'm not impressed with the tea here. I'll have to mention it to catering. Did you know Isabelle is coming back, by the way?'

'Oh, good,' Hannah murmured. She couldn't find the tea, her fingers were trembling, she almost knocked a cup off its saucer.

She turned away from Jopi so she wouldn't see.

It was the shock, she would say, *of waking suddenly.* With a pang of relief she saw the tea bags, which were where she'd put them, temporarily, on the computer table.

'She texted me to say she was returning, but she didn't say anything about meeting with Lucy – how it went.'

Hannah mumbled something in reply, manoeuvring saucers, spoons, pouring hot water onto a teabag.

'One can only hope,' said Jopi. 'But really, it's you I want to talk about.'

'Me?'

'Yes, you – we haven't had any chance to catch up yet. And I want to know all about you! How is your book going? How is Thibaut? Are you planning to go away like last year? And why have you been avoiding everyone, while you're here?'

'I haven't,' Hannah said, passing a cup of tea to Jopi.

'Ah, dreadful!' Jopi said, taking a sip. 'What *do* they put in these tea bags – floor sweepings? I really will have to have a word with the manager. And yes, you have,' she went on. 'No one has seen you at breakfast, or lunch, or in the evenings.'

Hannah sat on the bed. 'I went out yesterday evening,' she said. 'I saw Anton, and Karl. And Neville,' she added.

'Yes, Neville,' Jopi said, sniffing the tea, 'such a coincidence – you two being at the same conference. He came to see me, you know?'

'I believe so.'

'He wants to give an extra lecture, in Anton's place. Something about rewriting the past? He said he would be drawing on his childhood experiences. And yours too.'

Hannah's cup shook a little. She put it down on the locker.

'So I thought we should talk about that. Whether you are comfortable with having your childhood discussed in a public lecture.'

'Not really, no,' Hannah said, adding bitterly, 'But he seems determined to do it anyway.'

'I can always say no,' Jopi said.

Hannah thought about that, the effect it might have. When she didn't reply, Jopi said. 'What is it between you two? It's obvious to everyone that something's going on. At first I thought, ah, they have had an affair.'

'*Please.*'

'But the – what do you say? The vibrations didn't seem quite right. And then he came to ask me about the lecture, and I thought, *well, perhaps I should check with Hannah first.*'

Into the silence Jopi said, 'Is there anything you want to talk about?'

Hannah stared at her cup.

'You know you can talk to me, Hannah,' Jopi said.

Hannah looked at Jopi. Her face was creased with concern. The pattern on her trousers was humming-birds and cranes. The colours shifted and shimmered as Hannah looked at them, almost as though the wings were beating.

She put her cup down, clasped her hands together. 'Yes,' she said. 'There is something.'

Jopi sat back.

After another pause, Hannah said, 'You know Neville and I went to the same primary school – until we were eleven?'

Jopi nodded. 'He said so on the first night, yes.'

'At that time, I had a friend, a little girl called Joanna. She was in the same class as me, as was Neville – she lived on the same street.'

How could she describe *the street* to Jopi?

'In a – nicer house – further up – the children there didn't really play with children like me.'

She glanced at Jopi who nodded, although Hannah could tell she didn't understand. Not all countries suffered from the same brutal class distinctions and prejudices as England. But she didn't want to have to explain the whole social background to Jopi, her whole childhood.

'Anyway – behind the houses there was a stretch of woodland, leading down to a reservoir. We weren't supposed to play there – all the grown-ups thought it was dangerous, but – well, we couldn't play in Joanna's garden, and my house didn't *have* a garden.'

She paused again, remembering all the times she'd gone to Joanna's gate. Sometimes Joanna would be playing with Alison or Susan, and then Hannah would walk away, knowing she couldn't join in. Sometimes, even when the blind was up and Hannah could see her at the window, she wouldn't come down.

Once, Jo's mother had come out instead.

'Joanna's doing her homework now, dear,' she said. 'You'll have to come back another time.'

There was no question of Hannah being invited in. Was that because of her mother, or because of Hannah herself?

She didn't say any of this to Jopi.

'So we played in the Wild – that was what we called it. It seemed magical to us, despite the danger. Or because of it. I don't think children play out like that now, do they?'

'Unsupervised? Probably not,' Jopi said.

'We climbed, played hide and seek, and invented all kinds of games – or Joanna did. One of them was that we had to make stepping stones in the water using various things we found in the Wild. We had to make it hard for the other one to cross them, and we gained points if they fell in. I fell in a lot,' she laughed a little, but Jopi's face was grave.

It's not slippy, Jo's voice said, *Jump!*

She'd had to get all the way around the reservoir without using the path, to stay in the game. If she got her feet wet, or slipped into the water, the Others might grasp her ankles and pull her down. Then she would belong to them.

That was what they wanted, the Others. Company.

So she would leap from plank to stone, or a rusted railing that Jo had dragged into the water, grasping at branches or reeds on the banks, terror in her mouth, her bones, at every wobble or slip.

'Go on!' Jo would cry, from the bank. 'The stones aren't slippy!' when they were, or 'it won't wobble!' when it did. She'd skidded on the stones, scratched herself on brambles and thistles, slid into the mud at the reservoir's edge, clambered back on all fours. When it was Jo's turn she leapt easily from plank to stone, without faltering or stumbling. But Annie, always clumsy, fell in nettles, twisted her ankle, got her trainers soaked. She would return home muddy and injured, her skirt torn, knowing her mother would rant at her and slap her legs.

'Why you?' she always said, scrubbing at Annie's socks, her trainers, her shirt. She spat on a tissue and scrubbed at Annie's cheek, tore a comb through her hair. 'Why is it always you?'

Jopi was waiting, just as Hannah would wait for a client to speak. Hannah touched her throat, swallowed. When she started to speak the words tumbled out of her.

'You've probably guessed what happened. When it was my turn to make stepping stones Joanna fell in. And she didn't get out again. I don't know why - we only went around the edges - the water wasn't even that deep - and Joanna could swim - she was a good swimmer - not like me. I tried,' she said, her voice cracking. 'I tried to get her out, but she must have hit her head, or something. Caught her foot - they said her foot had caught—' Her voice disappeared.

Jopi's face was a picture of horrified sympathy.

'So I ran for help. That's where Neville came in. He was there. He used to follow us - I think he was lonely. He didn't have any friends, and we wouldn't let him play with us, so he just - hung around.'

Hannah closed her eyes, feeling inexpressibly weary. There was too much to explain. Everything led to something else.

'What did Neville do?' asked Jopi.

'I'm not sure, but I *think* he went down to the water, to try to help Joanna, while I ran to her house.'

Banging at the back door, then the front.

'I didn't think anyone was in at first, but then her brother answered - and I saw my mother coming down the street. She told Joanna's brother to call an ambulance and she followed me. And she managed to get Joanna out of the water – but by that time it was too late.'

'My God,' Jopi breathed, 'that's terrible – so terrible. And you were – how old? Eleven?'

'Ten – I was one of the youngest in my year – I wasn't eleven until the end of summer.'

The age of criminal responsibility.

'My God,' Jopi repeated. She stood up and paced.

'So that's what he wants to talk about? In his lecture?' her voice went up in disbelief.

'Well – yes, and no,' Hannah said.

Jopi sat down again. Hannah closed her eyes.

'OK,' she said. 'I told you Joanna invented games. One of them was called The Others. She said the Wild was full of them – these magical people, who were only half human. Some of them had antlers, or hooves. Humans were their enemies – we had hunted them almost to extinction. So they wanted revenge. They were always on the lookout for human children, to trap them, or drown them . . .'

She swallowed, remembering the terror of it, of the Others and the drowned girls. Then she glanced at Jopi and said, 'It was so real to me, all of it, I believed in it completely – or I wanted to. I think I would rather have lived in that magical world, than the world I did live in – you know?'

Jopi nodded, her face unreadable.

'Anyway, when all the questions started, and there were so many of them – they seemed to go on forever – I remember saying, at one point, *the Others did it*. And of course they asked, what others?' and my mother – she said – *there were no others, there was only Neville.*'

Jopi expelled all her breath at once. 'Aah.'

'Yes.'

'What happened - was Neville charged?'

'No he wasn't - there was no evidence - and the police couldn't make sense of my statement - I kept contradicting myself, I suppose - I hardly knew what I was saying in the end.'

'You were confused.'

'Yes.'

'You were a child - of course you were confused. We all know that a child's *truth* is very different from an adult's - the lines are different, the boundaries more blurred.'

'Yes,' Hannah said, bleakly.

'Hannah, you weren't to blame . . .'

'That's not how Neville sees it. I'm afraid he suffered a great deal from the investigation - and afterwards.'

Briefly she outlined what Neville had told her about his parents, his boarding school. Jopi shook her head in dismay. 'Ahh, God!'

Then she said, 'So - you think that's why he came here? To the conference?'

'Did you know him before?'

'Not really - he started communicating with me by email a while ago, about some article I'd written. I rather liked him - he always had something interesting to say, - and then he said he would be interested in giving a paper at this conference, and I thought, Why not?'

'Did he know I'd be here?'

'Well, yes - I asked you quite early on, if you remember - you think that's why he wanted to come?'

'I don't think he was surprised to find me here as he claimed. I think he . . .'

What should she say? *Tracked me down?*

'Looked me up, realised I was associated with you, and - well - here he is.'

'But why would he not contact you directly?'

Because I wouldn't have replied, Hannah thought. 'I don't know,' she said. 'It seems almost as though he wants this conference as a kind of – stage, where he can act out his – suffering.'

She'd almost said 'revenge'.

'But – what does he think he will achieve by it?'

My exposure? A scandal? Public condemnation? Hannah shook her head.

'It was a terrible thing – a tragedy – but it was no one's fault.'

'I don't think he sees it like that . . .'

'But he must! Anyone would! And in any case, it's in the past now, it's over. Although of course the past is never over. We should have a different word for it really, not *past* – just another dimension of the present.'

Hannah glanced up. A different tone had entered Jopi's voice. The older woman had stood and turned away from Hannah.

'Did you know I had a son?' she said.

'I – what?'

'Tobias – Tobi. He killed himself when he was seventeen.' Jopi's voice was flat.

'God, Jopi – I didn't know!'

'It was before I met you – two or three years before. Still too painful for me to talk about. Drugs, of course.' She turned, finally, and sat down.

'I'm so sorry,' Hannah said, inadequately.

'We tried everything – rehab, counselling. We wouldn't give him money when he wanted it, so of course he stole. One time he broke into a shop, armed with a knife, and threatened the owner. Which is why I decided to stop protecting him. I made him go through the criminal justice system. And then he killed himself.'

Jopi's eyes were closed. Her face had altered, as though the same skin had been draped over different bones. Hannah hardly knew what to say, how to respond.

Jopi had said, *we*, but Hannah had never known her to have a regular partner.

'Your husband?' she said, tentatively.

'Dieter, yes,' Jopi said. 'We split up soon afterwards.'

A world of suffering in those few words. And Hannah had only seen the colourful Jopi, her smile, her clothes. The bright halo surrounding a depth of human darkness.

'Jopi, I—'

'So you see,' Jopi said, opening her eyes. 'We all have two pasts – the one we speak about and the one we don't. And the one we don't speak about is the important one, no? The one that drives us. Isn't that the reason we're here, now? You, me and Neville – we are all here because of something unspeakable that has happened to us. We have devoted our lives to understanding how such things can happen, and what can be done to prevent them happening again. And above all, to understand how it might be possible – if it ever is possible – to move on?'

How indeed? Hannah thought bitterly. Had she not done everything she possibly could to *move on?*

'We feel that if we can save one single child from becoming a drop in an ocean of tragedy, then we might be able to forgive ourselves, and it might all be worthwhile, no?'

Hannah nodded, uncertainly.

'That's what you and I want at any rate – to save children from themselves – and from the world. But what does Neville want?'

Revenge, Hannah thought. but suddenly it seemed more complicated than that.

Jopi said, 'Perhaps we should ask him?'

'I don't think so.'

'How else will we find out?'

Hannah didn't want to find out. She was already beginning to regret this conversation, but Jopi seemed determined to press it through to some kind of conclusion.

'What does he think he stands to gain?' she pondered aloud.

Nothing, Hannah thought. Apart from humiliating her. But then she remembered what Thibaut had said. 'Perhaps he – wants to be heard – given a platform, maybe?'

'And you think we should not give him that platform?'

'I didn't say that.'

'What are you afraid of, Hannah?'

So many things swarmed into Hannah's mind that she couldn't speak. Her mother, Neville, losing Thibaut, the Drowned Girls. She shook her head.

'Are you afraid that people will judge you – for being a child? For having a past?'

Yes, Hannah wanted to say. Jopi leaned forward in her chair and clasped Hannah's hands. Hannah flinched in surprise, but Jopi carried on as if she hadn't noticed.

'No one will judge you – you know why? Everyone in that lecture theatre will be too busy remembering their own unspoken pasts. We all have them Hannah – surely being therapists has taught us that? Look at you,' she went on. 'Look how far you've come – you should be proud!'

Hannah had never felt proud. Mainly she felt lucky, as though gifted, somehow, with the kind of luck that a fugitive has.

Jopi released her hands, and lifted her own hands as if holding an imaginary rope.

'See where you were at ten, and where you are now,' she said, 'Here,' she twitched one imaginary end, 'is the lonely, traumatised child. And here,' she twitched the other end, 'is Professor Rossier, who has made a new life for herself, in a different country, and risen to the top of a notoriously difficult profession! Don't you think people will be amazed? Don't you think they need to know that such a trajectory is possible – these people who work with troubled children every day? But,' she went on, as Hannah started to speak, 'if you don't want it to happen, I understand – really I do. Just say the word, and I will stop Neville giving his lecture.'

Hannah stared at the imaginary rope. 'I – don't know – I think – if you stop the lecture, it won't stop Neville.'

'No?'

'He's determined to make himself heard somehow. He's come this far . . .'

Jopi nodded slowly, lowering her hands. 'So – in that case – what we have to do is to make sure you are heard too.'

'What do you mean?'

'I mean – it shouldn't only be his voice in the lecture theatre.'

Hannah felt a sudden qualm.

'What if that session is not a lecture, but a forum – a plenary, in fact, where a group of people reflect on the themes of the conference and relate them to their own experiences?'

Hannah started to say she didn't think Neville would agree to that, but Jopi was pacing again.

'I can ask Maryam – she will give us a different perspective. I will introduce the topic, and chair the discussion – mediate if necessary.'

'opi—' Hannah began, but Jopi carried on.

'Don't you see, Hannah - it's the only way for you and Neville to discuss your story objectively! So that it doesn't turn into one man's personal agenda!'

Objectively, Hannah thought.

'We're all so focussed on trying to hide or re-write our unspoken stories that we forget what we can learn from them - what they teach us about ourselves. Everyone who is interested in the criminal justice system needs to know your story!'

No! Hannah thought.

Jopi stopped pacing and sat again, taking Hannah's hands once more. 'Do say yes, Hannah. I will be there with you, supporting you. And - if you talk about your childhood tragedy, I will talk about my son.'

Her eyes were actually glistening. Hannah had never seen Jopi cry. She felt a pit of dread opening in her. It had been there all the time, waiting for her to fall in.

'Surely it's better,' Jopi insisted, 'than just letting Neville say whatever he wants?'

Hannah removed her hands from Jopi's. Part of her mind was attempting to imagine the scene before it happened, the probable outcome. The rest was protesting at the thought of being on any kind of platform with Neville.

'Hannah - what is it?'

'I just think - I don't want to have to defend myself, that's all.'

'That's not what this is about.'

'I don't want it to turn into some kind of slanging match.'

'It won't!'

'And I don't want—' She stopped.

'Yes?'

Hannah sighed. 'I don't want to - say the wrong thing.'

She'd known, since Joanna's death, that it was very, very dangerous to say anything. When she'd stopped speaking, all the people, all the questions had gone away.

'I understand,' Jopi said. 'The child in you has been silenced for so long she no longer knows how to speak. But now it's time to let her out, Hannah – and give her a voice!'

I'm giving you a chance to let the trapdoor open, Hannah. The trapdoor you've kept locked all these years. With little Annie on the other side.

But neither Jopi nor Neville knew what little Annie was like.

'Don't you see,' Jopi was saying, 'the context changes everything! You're not going to simply allow Neville to tell your story – you will have an equal chance to speak. You will be there with me, and Maryam, and many other people who will want to hear you, Hannah, who will *be on your side!*'

On your side. It sounded like combat, rather than a forum. Hannah versus Neville.

But she didn't want to fight, she wanted to run away.

Another thought came to her. 'I don't want anyone to write about this,' she said, 'in some journal. Or anywhere else!'

'Of course not,' said Jopi, 'we will make that clear from the start. It will be a forum where people discuss their personal experience, not an academic lecture. There will be no Open Access.'

Hannah looked at her warily. But she could see that Jopi was right – the context did change everything. if Neville resorted to attacking her he would rapidly lose the sympathy of the audience.

'I will personally make sure that nothing is printed without the express permission of all participants,' Jopi said.

Hannah expelled all her breath slowly. The silence stretched out uncomfortably. Jopi waited. Finally Hannah looked up. 'OK,' she said. 'I'll do it.'

XX

'I CAN PHONE Neville now,' Jopi said.

'No, *please*,' said Hannah.

'OK, I'll text him.'

'He might say no,' Hannah said.

'I'm not *asking* him,' said Jopi, laughing. 'It's my conference, after all!' She tapped into her phone.

The forum would be first thing, she said, at ten. Before Hannah's lecture – if Hannah felt up to that?

Hannah didn't, of course, but she nodded wearily. It would take its course now, she thought. Everything. Like some Greek play.

They always ended well.

Jopi wanted to discuss more details, but Hannah had had enough. 'You decide,' she said. 'I'll do whatever you want.'

Then Jopi asked if Hannah would eat in the restaurant, and Hannah realised with a small shock that it was nearly 7pm. But she wasn't hungry, and she definitely didn't want to see Neville again.

Jopi read her thoughts. 'You're worried about Neville being there,' she said. 'But I think he's made his own arrangements. And in any case,' she said, putting a hand on Hannah's arm. 'You have to stop hiding now.'

Her eyes were luminous with conviction. But Hannah said she needed to go through her lecture again. She would order a snack in her room.

'You're not eating properly,' Jopi chided, but at the look on Hannah's face, she stopped.

'*Bien*,' she said. 'I will go. I will email you the details.'

'Thank you,' Hannah said. Jopi hovered for a moment, assuring Hannah that she was doing the right thing, the best thing, and it would be good. Then finally, she left.

Hannah sank down on the bed, hardly able to believe she'd agreed to the forum.

What would Neville say about her?

What would she say?

Would he give up, afterwards, or continue to pursue her?

The pit of dread was still there, in her stomach, a trembling, as though everything would fall through. It wasn't just Neville, something else was disturbing her.

Jopi.

Did you know I had a son?

Ah, God.

The boundaries had shifted between them, because of their confessions. It was if Jopi had staked a claim on her somehow, and she didn't want it. She didn't want to be moved onto this unfamiliar terrain.

Intimacy. She only knew how to avoid it.

She stood suddenly, agitated, and stepped towards the window.

Outside, a light from a plane winked its way across a darkening sky. The lamps in the forecourt below illuminated the leaves of the plane trees. Hannah stood by the window, staring out, as in childhood she had stared at the lighted windows belonging to other people's lives.

Once, her mother had stood in Hannah's doorway, not saying anything, just watching, until Hannah had looked up.

She wasn't speaking then, not even at home, but her eyes had asked the question, *what?*

And her mother had said, 'Is there something - anything - you're not telling me?'

Hannah could sense, beneath the question, her mother's fear. She could almost smell it. She'd shaken her head, but her mother had said, 'You can tell me, Hannah.'

She couldn't speak. Her throat, the muscles in it, seemed paralysed. She'd shaken her head again, staring at her mother, until she'd finally turned away.

Her silence had saved them both. But now she was expected to break that silence.

The hotel room was dark. Hannah fumbled to switch the lamp on. She couldn't afford to brood, she had work to do.

What had Jopi said? The forum would come first, then her lecture.

That wouldn't give her much time to alter her notes, to respond to some of the things that might be said. That *he* might say.

It might run over time, there would be questions. She might be forced to go for coffee.

She couldn't predict what would happen - she who had turned planning into an artform, as though her life depended on it. She couldn't depend on it now.

Hannah opened her laptop and sat, staring at the screen. *Think.*

She searched for the file containing her lecture, then sat staring at the words as if willing them to say something else, something illuminating, that would make everything all right.

Did he want her to beg his forgiveness? Would that be enough?

How could she write anything until she knew what had been said? And then there would be no time.

Hannah leaned her head on the lid of her laptop. Closing her eyes, she could see a green tangle of wood and fern. The childhood world she'd lost. Where everything was twisted, fallen, split at the root. Where ivy fed off the trunks of trees and bindweed choked the life out of shrubs, and fungi sprouted in rotten wood.

What had happened there, in that world, felt like survival.

She missed it. She missed The Wild. She missed the child she was there, the one who followed different rules.

XXI

HANNAH WOKE, STARING at her digital clock, which said, improbably, 09.07.

No.

The forum was at ten.

She'd stayed up late, rewriting parts of her lecture, then lying awake with a stream of increasingly unfocussed thoughts. And now she'd overslept.

Shit.

Everything came flooding back to her, lunch with Neville, the conversation with Jopi, the forum.

Shit, shit.

With a groan she swung her legs out of bed and headed for the shower, twisting her hair into a knot so she wouldn't have to wash it. She wouldn't have time to wash it.

She hadn't eaten last night, and there would be no time for breakfast. Fortunately, there was coffee in her room. She put the kettle on, then went to the shower, turned it to cold and stood, gasping, under it.

Because she was late, nothing worked. She banged her toes into the bed frame, and was temporarily blinded by pain. When she could see again, through watering eyes, she realised she hadn't charged her phone and hastily plugged it in, then got dressed in the slate-blue suit with the cream shirt, before remembering she'd worn the cream shirt yesterday, and changed into the white.

She wasn't happy with the white, it made her look washed-out. But she hadn't packed much clothing. She would have to pin her hopes on blusher.

Before starting on her make-up, she made a coffee, strong and black, then spilled several drops down the white shirt.

Shit, shit, shit.

And the day hadn't even started yet.

Could she phone Jopi and call it off – say she couldn't do the forum?

She could if her phone was working, but it still wasn't charged, and the one in her room only connected to reception.

Hannah stripped off the white shirt. She would have to wear the cream one again.

Would anyone notice?

Tough.

Somehow, the lipstick she'd applied yesterday looked all wrong today, as though her complexion had changed over-night. She stared in despair at the mirror. She looked as she felt, exhausted and desperate.

9.42. No time to start again.

Jopi had said she would send an email, but Hannah's laptop seemed to be updating itself and her phone was nowhere near charged. And she desperately needed to grab something from the café. Rapidly, she bundled papers, pen drive and room key into her bag, then set off at a pace towards the lift.

She was in luck at the café, no queue and some sweet pastries left. It was not her preferred breakfast, but right now she needed sugar. She took the pastry with her, wrapped in a napkin, and ate most of it on the way to the theatre, dusting crumbs from her suit, hoping the pastry wouldn't cling to her teeth.

Already she could hear a buzz of voices. As she entered the

lecture theatre she realised it was almost full. The layout on the stage had changed, there were four seats at a table. Neville was in one of them, talking earnestly to a short, slightly squat woman who sat down next to him. She must be Maryam, Dr Abimbola. Jopi stood near the screen issuing some last-minute instructions to Pierre (or was it Michel?).

Hannah glanced at the clock. 9.59. By some miracle she'd made it. Hoping she looked more composed than she felt, she ascended the steps to the stage.

'I preferred his earlier work,' Neville was saying.

'But that was entirely derivative of a different director – Amaka Igwe – do you know her?'

'I can't say I do.'

'I was at school with her, in Enugu – she was a wonderful film-maker – but she didn't get half the credit she deserved.'

'Isn't that always the way? Well, I'll certainly look her up – I'm always happy to add to my list of great African directors – ah – here she is!'

He flung his arms out as though preparing to embrace Hannah, although the expression on his face suggested otherwise. 'We're just having a fascinating discussion about African film and film-makers!'

Hannah could contribute nothing to this particular subject. She pulled out her chair, nodding at Dr Abimbola, who had a broad, beautiful, face, and cropped grey hair.

'Who's *your* favourite director?' Neville asked.

'I never seem to find time for films,' Hannah said, smiling apologetically at Maryam.

'Well, you *should*,' Maryam said, raising her eyebrows, 'film is the gallery of the soul.'

'That's such a great line!' Neville said.

Already, it seemed, he had ingratiated himself with Maryam.

Hannah adjusted her seat, took out her spectacles and a notebook from her bag, although notes would hardly be useful here. She was acutely conscious of more people filing in. Her heart thumped erratically and her head hurt. She adjusted her spectacles, took them off, wiped them and adjusted them again as Jopi hurried over. She was wearing the palazzo trousers with the brilliant pink jacket, and huge earrings.

'*There* you are – I was quite worried! Did you get my email?'

Hannah didn't want to admit she'd forgotten to charge her phone. 'I don't think so,' she said.

'Ah, the internet here! So unreliable! Well, have you all met?

'We have,' said Neville, although no one had introduced Hannah to Maryam.

'So, I thought I would introduce the session, then since Neville initiated this whole thing he could go first. Is that OK with you, Neville?'

Neville raised his shoulders and pulled the corners of his mouth down. 'If that's OK with everyone else. I really don't mind.'

Hannah couldn't look at him.

'*Bien*. Neville will tell his story and then Hannah will tell hers. Maryam, you will make your own contribution, and I will chair and field any questions. Is everyone ready? Michel?'

Michel hurried over and clipped a small microphone to Hannah's jacket.

'Now you have to say *testing, testing*,' Jopi joked. Then, louder, 'Hello? Is everyone here? Can I ask you all to take your seats please? The session is about to begin.'

Hannah fiddled nervously with the clip. Her mouth was dry. She didn't want to look up, at Neville, or Jopi, or the sea of faces in the auditorium. But she caught Maryam's eye and the other woman smiled warmly at her. Hannah was so startled she almost forgot to smile back. Then she was startled again as Jopi rapped a microphone on the table, making a percussive echo.

The noise in the lecture theatre died down.

'Ha! That is a good sound, yes?' Jopi said, pleased with herself. 'Well, it's wonderful to see so many of you here at this time in the morning! So many shiny, happy faces!'

A murmur of laughter from the room.

'You weren't up *too* late last night I hope? Well, at any rate, you've got yourselves here and that's good.'

She adjusted her enormous spectacles.

'Today, we have something different for you. But what am I saying – this whole conference is *something different* – that's why you're all here!'

Another appreciative murmur, and scattered applause.

'I created this conference for that reason. Because we are not just therapists – we are also people – parents and lovers and sons and daughters and friends. We come from many different nationalities and backgrounds and we all have our personal experiences and memories that colour, every day, what we professionally do.

'So while we have listened to many excellent lectures so far, I thought that this could be a space to talk about our individual journeys – to map out the secret roads that brought us here. The journeys we do not speak about, but keep to ourselves. I have called this session, *Histoires Cachées*, because it is the hidden history that makes us who we are.'

Jeremy Kyle for academics, Hannah thought. She'd always deplored this public confessional mode of entertainment that was so popular, it seemed, with everyone else.

'So when I learned that two of the speakers at my conference had a particular connection that I knew nothing about before I invited them here – I saw an opportunity to explore these hidden histories.

'I must stress that whatever is said in this session is *personal* – it cannot be printed or used in any way without the speaker's *express permission*. You will have to apply directly to them. Anyway – enough. You've met all the speakers here before, but we are very pleased to welcome again, Dr Neville Weir, Professor Hannah Rossier, and Dr Maryam Abimbola.'

A round of applause. Neville and Maryam nodded and smiled, Hannah could barely bring herself to look up. Her stomach hurt. She wished she hadn't eaten that pastry. She could feel, in a moment of terror, the old sensation of her throat closing as it had in childhood, when she'd been unable to speak, to defend herself. Surely that wouldn't happen now?

There was a bottle of water in front of her on the table. She unscrewed it and took a tentative sip, feeling the muscles work as she swallowed.

'It was Dr Weir who first proposed speaking at this session, so I thought he might like to begin. Neville – why don't you tell us how you know Professor Rossier?'

Neville began at once, without looking at Hannah. 'We were at school together – primary school, which, in England, is where you go until you're eleven, when you move to some kind of secondary school.'

'And were you friends, at school?'

'Not friends exactly – it was still that era – the early 1980s – when boys and girls didn't play together much. Not in northern, working-class towns at any rate.'

He started to say something else, then stopped. Jopi had to prompt him.

'Why don't you tell us the nature of your connection to Professor Rossier, then?'

Neville looked at Jopi. 'I guess you could say I used to follow her around.'

Us around, Hannah thought. *Me and Joanna*. But Neville continued. 'I didn't have many friends, neither did she – apart from one little girl called Joanna – who would sometimes play with her and sometimes not. And when she didn't, Annie – Professor Rossier – looked so – lost.'

Hannah felt a flow of heat. This was intolerable. She thought of interrupting, but Jopi said, 'You liked her.'

'I did,' Neville said, and the heat burned in Hannah's face. She lowered it quickly. 'But it was entirely unrequited – she wouldn't have anything to do with me at all!'

Bastard, Hannah thought, as a ripple of sympathetic laughter ran around the room.

'Every playground is full of unrequited love,' Maryam said, smiling, and Hannah shook her head at the table.

'It so is,' said Neville. 'Anyway, Annie and Jo, as we called them—'

Hannah squirmed.

'—lived on the same street, while I lived on a housing estate on the other side of a stretch of wild ground. We weren't really supposed to play there, but that's where Annie and Jo played – so that's where I would go to look for them, and watch them from a distance.'

'Now you sound like a stalker,' Maryam said, and there was uneasy laughter. Neville smiled.

'Maybe so,' he said. 'Really, I only wanted to be included in their games, in their friendship – but maybe that's what a stalker would say.'

The laughter was less uneasy now.

'Did you try to play with them?' Jopi asked. 'Or did you just follow them, and watch?'

'No, I did try, a few times at least. They always drove me away. Sometimes they threw things. Jo, especially, was quite fierce. But Annie would always follow her lead.'

Hannah started to contradict him, but Maryam said, 'They *threw* things?'

'Sticks and stones – you know the old rhyme – *sticks and stones may break my bones, but names will never hurt me?*'

Jopi and Maryam looked blank.

'No? Well it's a saying in England. They do hurt, though, sometimes, the names.'

He smiled pensively. There was a sympathetic hush. Hannah tried to catch Jopi's eye. 'I'm sorry—'she began, but Jopi lifted her hand.

'Hannah is right,' she said, unexpectedly. 'We need to press on a bit, to the crucial part. Neville will tell it from his point of view. But then, Hannah, it will be your turn.'

Hannah subsided, but felt her rage and loathing flare again as Neville said, 'Just setting the scene, you know, providing a little context.'

'Why don't you tell us what happened,' Jopi said, 'that made you decide to follow your friend – sorry – schoolmate – all the way here, to this conference, so many years later.'

'Sure,' Neville said, and there was a moment of compressed silence before he went on, 'the event you're referring to was actually a terrible tragedy. There was a reservoir, on the wild land where we played, and the little girl, Joanna, drowned in it.'

There was a shocked murmur from the audience. Hannah lowered her face still further.

'I was there,' Neville said. 'I was just making my way down

to the reservoir when I saw Hannah here, coming up the bank. She'd scraped all her hands and knees climbing through the bracken, she seemed distressed. I asked her what was wrong and she didn't answer – she just ran away from me. So I clambered down that bank to see what had happened and I thought I could see something in the water.'

Another murmur. Hannah kept her head lowered.

'Imagine how I felt,' Neville said, 'when I realised it was Jo in there.' He took his glasses off, and pinched the bridge of his nose.

There was absolute silence.

'I waded in,' he said, his voice now thick with emotion. 'I tried to get her out. But she was too heavy for me – so I – just stayed there, holding on—' He stopped as if overcome.

Hannah could see it all as he described it, Joanna's hair billowing out in the water, her eyes looking at Neville with that dead grey look Hannah had seen so often in her dreams. Or was she face downwards?

Or was she fighting him, with the last of her resistance, as Neville held her down?

That was what Hannah's mother had suggested to the police.

'I don't know how long I was there, holding on to her – I remember my main feeling was that I mustn't let go – so I just stayed there until Annie – Hannah – returned with her mother. And Hannah's mother, Mrs Price, managed to get Jo out. She tried to resuscitate her – but of course it was too late by then.'

He stopped and shook his head, brushing his eyes briefly. Maryam leaned forward. 'That must have been a terrible experience for you.'

'All my life,' Neville said, his voice cracking. 'Ever since that day, I've wondered what might have happened if I'd got there just a few seconds earlier—' His voice disappeared.

Hannah could feel the weight of sympathy for him in the room like a heavy blanket. Tension built in her throat. Jopi said, 'But that wasn't the end of your ordeal, was it?'

'No,' Neville said. 'No it wasn't. Soon after that, the police came, and the questioning began. And in the course of that questioning it became clear that the police were trying to *put the blame on me!*'

A shocked moan, over which Neville said, 'It seems that someone, Hannah – or her mother – had given them that idea!'

Hannah broke in, 'That's *not*—' she started to say, but Jopi interrupted her.

'Hannah,' she said. 'You must let Neville speak. And then it will be your turn.'

And he did speak, very eloquently, about his mother's illness and death, the school he'd been sent to, how long it had taken him to get his life back on any kind of track, to get where he was today. He was fluent, voluble even. Hannah could hear herself being damned with every word.

'I lost touch with Hannah – Professor Rossier – for many years,' he continued. 'I didn't know what had happened to her, where she'd got to, what she was doing. I'd even read some of her articles without knowing who she was. Her name had changed, of course. It wasn't until I saw her photo in a medical journal that I began to think – and even then I couldn't be sure. But when I saw that Professor Rossier was the main speaker at this conference, I thought that at last there would be a way to find out. And so I came here.'

'Why?' asked Jopi.

'What?'

'You went to some trouble to get yourself invited to this

conference. I'm wondering now what you hoped to get from it. Why are you here?'

For the first time, Neville seemed disconcerted. He took his glasses off and replaced them. 'Well, in part, it was curiosity that made me come,' he said. 'to see if it really was who I thought it was. And to find out,' he went on, his voice gaining strength, 'what had happened to that little girl I knew, all those years ago.'

Liar! Hannah thought.

'Curiosity,' Jopi said. 'Pure and simple. Not any desire for disclosure? Or exposure? Or, perhaps, revenge? You don't want to make the person who caused so much suffering in your life, suffer in return?'

'No, no – of course not – absolutely not!'

Neville seemed outraged by this suggestion.

'I may have wanted to see her, yes – to talk things through. Closure, perhaps, not *dis*closure. It seemed to me that it would tie in perfectly to the themes of this conference, to try to achieve some kind of resolution, perhaps, to what happened.'

'Forgiveness, then,' said Maryam.

'I – forgiveness – is a big word,' Neville said. For the first time he had struck the wrong note, he was floundering. 'I'm talking about being accused, wrongly – being isolated – and cut off from all support, from my family . . .' His words trailed off as he looked at Maryam, then Jopi, then he seemed to recover. 'Understanding, perhaps, as a first step. I'd like to understand what happened to me. Perhaps Hannah might have something to say about that?' he attempted a smile, achieving only a kind of smirk.

'Well, let's find out, shall we?' Jopi said. 'Hannah, you've listened patiently to everything that's been said about you, about what happened in your childhood, to you and Neville, and Joanna, of course. But if we learn anything, as therapists, it's that there is always more than one side to a story – so now, perhaps, we should hear your side.'

Hannah could feel the force of so many eyes looking at her like a burning sensation on the surface of her skin. All she wanted to do was crawl away. She could feel the muscles of her throat closing. *Not this, not now,* she prayed.

'I . . . don't know that I have anything . . . to say,' she managed. There was a minor protest from the audience.

'Really?' said Jopi. You've just heard Neville accuse you of bearing false witness – isn't that the term? Of ruining his life, in fact . . .'

Neville started to speak, but Jopi held her hand up, silencing him.

'Are you saying that you agree with his interpretation of events?'

'I – not exactly – no.'

'Then, Hannah, you owe it to yourself to speak.'

Hannah looked at Jopi. The older woman's gaze was focussed and intent. Neville and Maryam and what felt like a thousand eyes from the auditorium were looking at her as well. She closed her own eyes briefly. The memory of trying to help Martin Hawkes to speak came into her mind.

She had given him a balloon and told him to blow against it, *pah, pah.*

She could hardly do that here.

'What did Joanna's death mean to you, Hannah?' Jopi asked.

Hannah could see Joanna's face when her mother had pulled her out of the water. She'd never seen a dead face before. It was like Joanna's face but altered, unmistakeably dead. Her eyes were staring beyond Hannah as if she'd finally seen one of the Others. The impression had been so strong that Hannah had glanced over her shoulder to check. There was a rope of weeds twisted in her hair. Joanna wouldn't have liked that, she was fussy about her hair. Whenever Alison or Susan were round they would spend a long time in front of the mirror, brushing one another's hair. Hannah had watched them from the bottom of the garden, through Joanna's bedroom window.

Hannah shook her head slightly, to dislodge the memories. Suddenly she stood up.

No one had asked her to stand, Neville had delivered his whole speech sitting down, but Hannah stood before everyone in the room. The silence was like a wall, the muscles in her throat like a clamp.

She swallowed, hard. Focussed on the blank wall at the back of the room, beyond all the faces.

'Everything Neville - Dr Weir - has told you is correct - more or less,' she said. Her voice shook, and the microphone magnified the tremor. 'Joanna was my friend, and she died when we were playing together. It was terrible - for everyone. I—' She closed her eyes. She had absolutely no idea how to go on. Then she said. 'Nothing has been the same, since that day.'

A hushed expectancy. Everyone was waiting. *Speak!* Hannah ordered herself.

'It . . . I—'

She tried again.

'We had a game, me and Joanna. Joanna made it up, and I . . . played along. She said that the Wild - where we played - was full of magical creatures. We called them the Others.'

She told the story, as she had told it to Jopi, about the Others, what they looked like, their skin the colour of silver birch, their hair like bracken, or moss. How they hated humans, who had taken their land and hunted them, so they hid, and tried to trap children or lure them into the reservoir.

'Part of the game was to find the Others,' Hannah said, nodding at the wall, 'although it was never quite clear what we would do if we found one, or who was hunting whom.' She smiled vaguely, remembering the stepping stones, all the times Joanna had rigged it so that Hannah had fallen in. Once she'd cut herself on a pipe that Joanna had hidden in the water, and had hobbled home, her foot bleeding. But she hadn't dared tell her mother about it – she'd bathed it herself with some antiseptic lotion from the cupboard. The foot had swollen and turned red and was really painful, but still Hannah hadn't told her mother. And by some miracle it had healed.

'That was how Joanna drowned,' she said. 'It was my turn to make stepping stones in the water – and Joanna was crossing them when she fell in.'

There was a murmur from the audience, whether of sympathy or censure, she couldn't tell. She went on, 'It couldn't have been as shallow as we thought it was, because she just – disappeared.'

Another murmur.

Should she tell them she'd tried to save Joanna, waded in? She hadn't in fact; she was too afraid of the drowned girls. And the Others.

'I ran for help,' she said. 'And that's when I bumped into Neville. Then my mother. It was my mother who got Joanna out of the water. But it was too late by then. And of course, the police came, and asked a lot of questions. But I never, at any time, put the blame on Neville.'

She turned to him then, as he sat, gazing up at her, his mouth slightly open.

'I'm asking you to believe that,' she said.

Neville's face flushed. 'Then why did they tell me you had?'

'I know,' she said, nodding. 'I know they did – now. And I realise why.'

Turning back to the audience she said, 'I remember being confused by all the questions – I just wanted it all to go away. But the police asked me the same things, over and over again. And so at one point, I said to them, the Others did it. and of course, they wanted to know who the Others were. And I couldn't tell them. And my mother said, 'There *were* no Others – there was only Neville.'

A groan rose from the auditorium.

Hannah turned again to Neville. 'I didn't explain it to them because I couldn't. I stopped talking altogether – I became electively mute, although it didn't feel like a choice at the time.'

Neville shook his head.

'I didn't know the police were questioning you. All I knew was that they'd stopped questioning me – for the time being. That was all I wanted to know. I didn't know anything about what happened to you after that summer – I didn't know you'd been sent to a special school – and I didn't know about your mother. I'm truly sorry about that.'

Hannah felt herself swaying a little as she stood, her knees trembling. She sat down. Neville started to speak, but Jopi said, 'Would it be fair to say, Hannah, that all your energies, at that time, were devoted to survival?'

Hannah nodded, vigorously. 'Yes, yes it would. My life had changed – I'd lost my best friend – I never played with anyone apart from Jo. At the end of that summer I went to a different school – away from my old neighbourhood – completely away. It set me apart – cut me off, from everyone I knew. When I was at home I had to stay in – to do my homework – my mother made sure I did it.'

She didn't mention that her mother had taken to locking her in, or her mother's cleaning job at the hospital, that meant she was out in the early evenings, so Hannah was alone, locked in her room.

'At the new school I didn't make any friends. I was too shy – too socially awkward – and from the wrong background.'

Impossible to imagine taking any of the girls from her new school, some of them the daughters of millionaires, back home to that street, to her mother.

'Ah, the English class system,' Jopi said. 'It has to be experienced to be believed. And what about your mutism? How long did that go on? How did people handle it, at your new school?'

Sitting in silence at the back of the classroom, all the other girls in groups.

'I guess,' she said, 'it was easier to stay that way.'

'And the teachers just accepted it?'

'Mostly – as long as I did my work – which I always did. And my mother had made them aware of the – particular circumstances.'

'So, you didn't speak at all, the whole time you were there?'

'Not at first.'

'What prompted you, in the end?'

She had learned, finally, begun to accept, that she was really good at certain subjects.

'I guess I realised I could answer the questions we were asked.'

'In class?'

'Yes.'

'Not socially?'

'No.'

One or two of the girls had made overtures towards her,

realising she was always first in class tests and examinations. But she didn't trust them.

'Interesting that you spoke first in public.'

'Yes.' Maybe that had been the start of the public persona she had developed. Professional Hannah.

'So here we have a case,' Jopi said, 'where the child is lucky enough to have a certain gift, that gives her a platform from which she can operate, and from which she can build her future career. Otherwise, who can say what might have happened?'

An image of the Drowned Girls rose in Hannah's mind. She shook her head.

'It sounds to me as though you might have been utterly lost,' Jopi said. 'Is that fair?'

Hannah nodded. 'Possibly,' she said, her voice strained.

'But Neville, tell us,' Jopi went on. What is your response to Hannah's side of the story now you've heard it? How much of it did you already know?'

Neville was gazing down at the table, at his broad, stubby hands. There was a long silence. 'Well,' he said, drawing the syllable out. 'Not all of it.' He didn't look up.

'And how do you feel about it? Is it what you expected to hear? Can you accept what she says?'

Neville leaned back, looking at Hannah. Hannah felt as though insects were crawling over her skin. 'What?' he said. 'That she didn't intend to hurt me? That she didn't know what was happening to me? Or that she's sorry?'

Hannah was transfixed by his gaze, his tone. The lecture theatre was absolutely quiet. Jopi spread her hands. 'All of the above,' she said.

Abruptly Neville shifted his gaze from Hannah. She almost sagged, as if he'd been pinning her to the wall.

'If that's what Hannah says,' he said, to Jopi, 'then I guess it must be true. Her version of the truth in any case.'

A ripple of protest from the forum.

'But I will add this,' he said, slightly more loudly. 'She says she didn't know what happened to me, and that may be true. It's always true,' he went on, as the protest increased, 'that the oppressor can turn a blind eye to the oppressed.'

A shocked murmur.

'But Hannah was a little girl,' Jopi protested, 'not some political dictator!'

'Oh, I know that,' Neville said. 'But even so.'

Maryam leaned forwards. 'It isn't clear to me,' she said, 'what the source of your resentment is. Are you blaming Hannah for what she did, as a little girl, or for what she said, or for not taking the trouble to find out the impact on you?'

Several people agreed.

'It's not *blame*,' Neville said, turning towards Maryam. 'No one's talking about *blame* here, are we? We're talking about different versions of events, different narratives, and how one narrative can supersede another. Which is always the case, throughout history. Isn't that what the Me Too movement was all about?'

Shocked protest from the auditorium.

'What?' asked Neville. 'Why is this different?'

Several people spoke at once. A woman with multiple piercings stood.

'Can I just say that I think it's wholly inappropriate to compare this case to the Me Too movement? Can I say that I'm *offended* by the appropriation of it – in this context?'

Loud agreement. Someone called out, 'As if men haven't appropriated enough!'

And the woman sat, the many hoops in her ears quivering.

Neville blushed furiously. 'Well, we're talking about gender-related abuse,' he said, 'what else would you call it? I was accused, basically because I was a boy. And friendless.'

A man stood up.

'Professor Ahmad?' Jopi said.

'Thank you. I just think we should not apply these terms, such as Me Too, to a story in which both children, it seems to me, are victims. If you use the term Me Too, then surely you are talking about blame?'

More agreement.

'No,' said Neville. 'I just said—'

Professor Ahmad spoke over Neville.

'Well, if you are *not* talking about *blame*, then you must be talking about forgiveness, don't you think?'

'Neville?' Jopi asked.

Neville's flush had faded to an unattractive blotching. 'That would depend on what you mean by forgiveness,' he said.

Professor Ahmad said, 'In Arabic, the word for forgiveness is the same as the word for freedom,' and he sat down again to a small outbreak of applause.

There was a heated, turbulent energy in the room. Hannah hardly dared breathe. *It was turning*, she thought. It was turning against Neville. Or he had turned them against himself.

An older woman wearing a sari stood up. 'I would just like to salute you both for speaking,' she said. 'It is always easier to discuss issues in impersonal terms, rather than exposing yourself to comment and possible censure.'

Neville nodded slowly, Hannah looked down again.

'I do feel, however, that I must also pick up on your comment about the Me Too movement. What we are talking about here is not deliberate abuse, surely? It seems to me, from what I've heard, that there was a tragic accident, the drowning, followed by a series of misunderstandings and miscommunications. Your story gives an insight into the ways in which the criminal justice system can go tragically wrong – and we can all learn from that, I think. But there was no question of deliberate intent, and therefore, there can, or should, be no blame. However, you've referred, just briefly, to the historical and political context, and I was wondering whether Dr Abimbola has anything further to say about that?'

She sat down into a sudden silence. Maryam leaned forwards.

'Thank you, Indah,' she said, 'and thank you, Hannah and Neville, for sharing this very personal, painful history with us here, today. You are right to suggest there is a political and cultural dimension to this case. We have two children, who for different reasons were isolated within their own communities. Why was this? Jopi has mentioned the class system in England. But also there does seem to be a gender issue involved – why was Neville following the girls and why did the police focus so intently on this?'

Neville started to speak, but Maryam held up her hand again. 'In my own case, I too, have a story to tell. It concerns my brother.'

She looked around the auditorium. 'I grew up in a village outside Enugu. My mother had many children who died early. So in my family there was just me and my brother, Abeo, who was five years younger than me. My mother was often either pregnant or sick and I was expected to look after my brother. On this particular day, he wanted to play football with his friends while I wanted to go to the shops with my girlfriends. So I allowed him to go on his own. That was the day he disappeared.'

There was a shocked silence. Maryam expelled her breath

in a long sigh. 'We all searched for him, everyone in the surrounding villages searched, but he was never found.' Her voice
shook, but she continued. 'Blame was put on different groups
in turn - firstly the Igbo tribes were accused of practising a
kind of tribal magic, or *muti*. But it was also known that a
group of white traffickers had been operating in the area. And
later it seemed that the government may have stirred hatred
between one tribal group and another for their own purposes.
Because that is how blame operates. From the top downwards.
We are all familiar with the idea of the scapegoat - someone
who is sacrificed when there are larger issues at stake.'

Many people responded to this. One older man mentioned
the case of Ken Saro Wiwa, also from Nigeria, who was executed ostensibly for organising the murder of four Ogoni
chiefs. But actually for leading a campaign against Shell.

'Exactly,' Maryam said.

A woman with dreadlocks said that her uncle had been
in prison for years in Indonesia, and the charges against him
kept changing.

Then everyone, it seemed, had some story of political
injustice or corruption. The atmosphere became heated and
emotional. Two people cried.

Once or twice Neville tried to speak but no one was listening. Hannah kept quiet, looking down at the mottled grain of
the table, sensing, with an element of disbelief, the tidal shifts
of emotion, and support.

Then the man with the horn-rimmed glasses stood. 'But -
can you tell us a little more about what happened about your
brother?' he said to Maryam. 'Was the mystery ever resolved?'

'No, never,' she said. 'There was no one to blame, never
any proof, and nothing was ever taken to court. So the fallout
was terrible. My father blamed my mother, my mother blamed

herself. I blamed myself. All my life, I will see him running down that dusty track, to play with his friends.'

Maryam turned towards Hannah. 'I was the same age as you – not quite eleven years old – and I still have nightmares about it. Somewhere inside me, I am still that traumatised child.'

Reluctantly, Hannah met Maryam's gaze. There was a moment of acknowledgement, recognition, then Maryam turned back to the auditorium.

'So where, in this case, does the blame really lie? In the economic situation that meant my mother never received any help for her ailments? In the gender politics that meant I, the daughter, had responsibility for my younger brother, when I was still a child? With the antagonism between tribal groups or the governments who benefited from it? Or with the traffickers?' she shrugged. 'Who knows? Nothing was ever proved – or ever will be. I have devoted my professional career to understanding the mechanics of blame and its displacements. Blame is like a shadow, or a shapeshifter. The more you look the less accurately you see. And when you think you have found the root of it, it disappears.'

For a moment Neville's gaze flickered towards Hannah and their eyes met. She looked quickly away.

Jopi seemed profoundly moved by Maryam's words. She leaned over and grasped her hands.

'Maryam,' Jopi said, in an emotional voice. 'Thank you so much for sharing your grief. I can only add my own story to this discussion.' She kept hold of Maryam's hands and spoke directly to her. 'My son, Tobi, was seventeen when he died of a drugs overdose. I had turned him into the police, hoping to prevent his illicit activities, but he killed himself.'

A groan from the audience. Sympathy had shifted again.

Jopi bowed her head. It was like a grotesque play, Hannah thought.

Jopi said, 'There has never been a day since that I do not remember him, and blame myself.'

Clamour. Everyone, it seemed, knew someone who had committed suicide. Everyone had suffered from the ensuing guilt, the sense of responsibility, that could not be appeased.

Maryam nodded slowly. 'So, this is my point,' she said. 'Who, in all these stories, do we blame? The drugs sellers? The economic forces that profit from trafficking? Inequalities in society? Or do we single out one person, often ourselves? Because blame is like a poison and it travels like water to the weakest point, the chink, in the individual or in the community. That's how many communities strengthen their cohesion, by singling out a victim.'

She turned finally to Neville. 'I suggest, that all these years, you have been blaming yourself for what happened, for all the difficulties and pain you endured, but because you needed to discharge some of that poison, Hannah has become your target. It is easier to blame her.'

Neville shook his head.

'I've already said this is not about *blame*,' he said, unnecessarily loudly. 'I'm talking about looking again at something that did so much damage, with the aim of bringing it into the open, into the clear light of day. Isn't that what we *do* as therapists? Isn't that what therapy is *for*? Haven't we spoken already, at this conference, about how young people can't always understand the consequences of their actions? We try to help them to take responsibility, but they can't do that without becoming more aware – we can't change a single thing while we remain too blinded by the past to even look at it!'

He shifted towards Hannah.

'That's what I'm doing here, Hannah – I'm giving you a chance to confront, in maturity, the consequences of what you did as a child!' his face had flushed again but his gaze held hers fiercely.

The response to this was immediate. Everyone spoke at once.

Had Dr Weir heard nothing that Dr Abimbola had said?

He surely didn't consider himself to be the arbiter of *truth* in this situation?

Was he not just reiterating the same pattern of blame and accusation?

Neville seemed increasingly baffled, outraged, frustrated. But he kept his peace until the woman with dreadlocks said that within every country, certain ethnic groups were singled out for blame. And within those groups the men blamed the women. It was the women who suffered, if not direct scape-goating, then the *repercussions* of blame.

And there was considerable applause.

For the first time, Neville stood. He seemed considerably agitated. 'Well, if we're on the subject of gender, I'd just like everyone here to consider the fact that in all these tragic stories, Dr Abimbola's, my own, and yours, Jopi, – the male child was the victim. Perhaps there is something to be said in all of this about what's happening to *men* in today's society. I'm just putting that out there.'

A roar of outrage. A young woman leaped up. She was very pale, with wispy hair. 'The politics of this case seem clear to me,' she said. 'As Dr Abimbola has said, blame has been displaced all the way along the line, until it falls on the most vulnerable party – the female child.'

More applause. Then the woman with dreadlocks stood again.

'Surely the point is that there is more than one victim in

all these stories? But while we're on the subject of gender, I would like to say that Dr Weir appears to be dominating this particular narrative. I would like Professor Rossier to speak again – to respond to everything Dr Weir has said.'

A chorus of assent. Jopi held her hand up again. 'Hannah?' she said. 'What do you think? Is there is a gender issue at the base of your story?'

Hannah was still staring at the table. She was acutely aware of Neville's rage and disappointment. *But what did he expect?* she thought. That was why she, Hannah, never said anything if she could help it. But Jopi had engineered a minor miracle for her and now she was asking her to speak. Hannah could hardly refuse.

She looked up.

'I think that each of these tragedies caused unbearable suffering – and as Dr Abimbola says, there are multiple issues underlying each of them—' She paused, as if unable to go on. 'But as far as what Neville – Dr Weir – has said about my own life being built on ignorance of his, I have to say that I agree with him—'

A rising murmur.

'Although I would add that to some extent we all live in a kind of willed blindness that enables us to survive. I did not understand the extent of his suffering – and he did not understand mine. As far as what he says about giving me a chance to confront, in maturity, the consequences of what I did as a child, I would say he has succeeded in that. I am now aware, to my sorrow, of the impact of what I did, or neglected to do. I would still say that none of it was deliberate – there was no *intent* to harm – although maybe, in the end, that's no excuse.'

She turned towards Neville, who sat gazing at her with a kind of petrified awareness, *like a rabbit in the headlights*. 'So now, what I would ask Dr Weir is, is that enough? And if not, please, tell me – what would be enough? What else can I can do for you here, now?'

A sudden hush descended. Neville was rocking slightly. He looked almost as though he might burst into tears.

'Nothing,' he said, heavily. 'There is nothing you, or anyone else can do.'

A sigh rose from the auditorium. Neville was gripping the desk as though it was a raft.

'People have spoken of forgiveness, of *moving on*. And I know where you're coming from – I really do. But is that what we're really talking about here?' he said, looking into the auditorium. 'All the people you mention, all the histories – is *forgiveness* what you want? Really?'

Maryam leaned forwards and said, 'In my country, we have a saying, *the only thing we owe one another is forgiveness.*'

'Well, that's great,' Neville said. 'But surely, for forgiveness to happen, something has to change. And essentially, nothing has changed here, has it? Because to *move on* would require a kind of emotional honesty that I don't feel we have achieved, or can possibly achieve, here, in this forum.'

Again, everyone spoke at once. The woman with dread-locks accused him of vindictiveness.

How could Neville judge Hannah's honesty, or lack of it?

Was he revelling in his role of victim?

Neville looked from one speaker to another. His face was blotched, his mouth partially open. Hannah felt almost sorry for him.

But when an older man said that all Dr Weir had succeeded in doing was exposing his own emotional immaturity, Neville pushed his chair back and stood. 'I'm not listening to this,' he said, Jopi stood too. 'Wait, please,' she said, then turning to the lecture theatre, and knocking on the table she said, more loudly, '*Please!*'

Neville paused for a moment, but then continued to leave, scraping his chair, turning his back on them, making his clumsy exit from the theatre. Jopi looked after him, then at Hannah, then back to the theatre with an apologetic grimace and a sigh.

'I'm so sorry about that,' she said. 'Obviously, the work of coming to terms with the past is always painful. It's a lifelong process. I want to thank you all for listening,' she said. 'And I want to thank my colleagues, Professor Rossier, Dr Weir and especially Dr Abimbola, for sharing her own story with us, in such a moving way. Last night, I wasn't sure about doing this session, but now I'm glad I did. I think in some ways it has been the most valuable of the whole conference. So I want to thank you, all of you, for participating.'

There was a moment of silence, then the applause began. Maryam joined in, then Jopi. Hannah could hardly believe that she'd survived the session relatively unscathed. She joined in the applause. They were all applauding one another.

Jopi announced that the final lecture of the conference would be given by Professor Rossier in less than fifty minutes. 'We have over-run, as usual,' she said, smiling at Hannah. 'But I'm sure you'll all be very keen, after this session, to hear what Professor Rossier has to say.'

The applause went on as they left their seats. Several people tried to make their way to the front, and Jopi had to announce again that since there was hardly any time before the next lecture, perhaps they could save their questions for then?

Hannah couldn't wait to get out. She felt as though she'd survived a trial by fire, even though, unexpectedly, it hadn't burned her at all. As she maneuvered her way out of the theatre, she heard Jopi calling her. She was surrounded by a crowd of delegates, but waving at Hannah.

'I'll come to you, before your lecture, if that's OK?' she called.

It wasn't, not really. Hannah wanted to say there would be no time, and she didn't want the company, or any post mortem on the forum. But there was too much distance between herself and Jopi, too many people, to say anything without shouting. So she smiled and nodded, hurrying away.

XXII

HANNAH TOOK THE stairs to her room. She didn't want to be trapped in the lift with anyone from the forum.

But she was accosted as she reached the second floor, by a youngish man with straggling hair and John Lennon glasses.

'I was hoping you might sign this for me,' he said, holding out a copy of Hannah's book, *Subject Positions*.

She couldn't place his accent. East European, perhaps? How had he managed to find her?

'I really admired the way you resisted allocating blame in there,' he went on as she signed her book, *best wishes, Hannah Rossier*, without asking his name. 'That must have been so hard!'

Hannah wouldn't be drawn in to a discussion. She made her excuses, backing away, hurrying up the stairs before he could follow her to her room. How ironic would it be if she acquired some kind of celebrity status from all this?

It was the last thing she wanted.

She let herself in, leaning against the door, closing her eyes. Her legs felt weak – was she trembling? Or was it just the stairs?

She had maybe forty minutes to make changes to her lecture notes. Forty minutes, before she stood before them all, and Neville, again. What on earth could she say? Thoughts were fizzing in her brain, Neville, Jopi, Maryam, Neville again.

When he'd said, *the male child was the victim*, Hannah had seen feet dangling in the middle of a room. She couldn't even think, at first, what the image was, and then she realised.

Danny Millfield.

He had moved from job to job, had a couple of kids with different partners and then, aged 20, had hung himself from the light fitting in the temporary accommodation provided for him by the council.

No note.

What would it have said if he had left one?

Over the years, more than one of her clients had taken that way out. She'd learned to put a distance between herself and the pain. Perhaps it was because she'd met him so early in her career that the memory remained with her. Danny Millfield. Not Michael, not Martin, but Danny.

But, the thing was, she'd never actually *seen* Danny hanging in that room. The image of it had formed in her mind, vividly, when she'd heard what had happened to him. It had turned into a memory that was as real to her now as any of her own.

What did that say about memory?

Hannah expelled her breath, realising that she'd been holding it. There was a band of tension around her ribs. She recalled Neville's face just before he left the theatre.

Whatever she said in her lecture, it had better be good.

She peeled herself away from the door and walked towards the computer. What could she say that wouldn't make the situation worse? She stared at the blank screen for a moment, then turned it on and searched for her file.

A few minutes later, someone knocked at her door.

Jopi.

She'd said she would come. But Hannah wasn't ready. She would have to put her off.

As the knocking came again, louder, she reluctantly got up. 'Coming,' she said, and opened the door.

Neville bowled straight past her. She had to step backwards to get out of his way.

'What was all *that* about?' he said.

Hannah stared at him in dismay. He looked dishevelled, his face still blotchy. She thought she could smell something on him, but he would hardly have had time to start drinking.

'What was that - some kind of blood sport?'

'Neville—'

'Girl power - let's all gang up together!'

'I don't think—'

'What a set up - did you *ask* her to set it up?'

'Neville,' Hannah said firmly. 'I don't have time for this. I have to prepare my lecture.'

'Ah yes - your lecture!' His glasses gleamed, he was perspiring. He had moved so he was standing between Hannah and the door. *Never let the patient block your exit* - it was one of the first things she'd learned.

'I can't wait to hear that. Are you going to finish the hatchet job?'

'I really don't—'

'How do you get away with it? Always the victim, always the good little girl?'

Hannah took a step forwards, and slightly to one side, as though she might step round him to the door. 'I'm going to have to ask you to leave.'

'But I've only just got here,' Neville said.

He had a manic look in his eye, Hannah began to wonder whether he really was deranged. *Where were panic buttons when you needed them?* She thought of pushing him to one side in an aikido manoeuvre, getting past. And then what? Would she shout for help in the corridor?

'And I've only got one question to ask.'

'Well?'

'You thought I'd said, *what have you done?* Remember? When I saw you running away from the reservoir, all those years ago. So what I'd like to know now is, what did you think I meant?'

Hannah stared at him. The little pulses in her temples started throbbing.

'I don't know what you—'

'Yes, you do,' Neville said. 'I couldn't even remember saying it, but you said you remembered it clearly. *What have you done?* So, now I *am* asking, Hannah - what *had* you done?'

Hannah turned away from him. She stared out of the window, towards the mountains. Everything that had happened had been moving towards this moment here, now.

Behind her Neville said, 'Everyone knew Joanna wasn't all she was cracked up to be. She certainly wasn't the plaster cast saint people turned her into after her death. All those little shrines to her along the street, the memorial service, the newspaper articles - how she went shopping for the elderly, organised a litter pick-up, cured the blind and the lame - did everything, in fact, apart from rising from the dead. But you and I, Hannah, both know that wasn't the full story. We know that Joanna could be a little bitch, don't we?'

Hannah didn't turn or look at him. She could hear him pacing now, behind her.

'I always used to wonder why you played with her at all,' he continued. 'She treated you like dirt - she wouldn't have anything to do with you at school, remember? And she made you wait at the bottom of her garden.'

'That's enough,' Hannah said, faintly.

'All the games you played – they were *her* games, weren't they? Games where you ended up falling, hurting yourself, soaking wet – how many times did she get you into trouble at home? Weren't you more of a skivvy than a friend? Or a personal slave? Or a – what do you call it – a whipping-boy? Funny, they don't have that name for girls, but they should. Were you Joanna's whipping-girl, Hannah?'

Slowly, Hannah turned. Neville seemed taken aback by the expression on her face.

'You don't know anything about my friendship with Joanna,' she said, very quietly.

'No? Well, why don't you tell me?'

Hannah stared at him so intently she could see the minute contractions of his pupils. She could feel him becoming less certain, beginning to quail. *Yes,* she thought. *You think you know me.*

'What's this really about, Neville?' she said. 'You're not happy with the way the forum went? Is that it? Were you expecting more sympathy? Do you want me to do some kind of penance? Stand up in my lecture and heap ashes on my head, crying *mea culpa, mea culpa?* What can I say, or do, that will *actually* make you feel better?'

Neville was looking at her now with wary loathing. She wondered if it was mirrored on her own face, and attempted to soften her expression.

'Because I know that you were hurt, badly – you really suffered, but there's nothing I can do about that. Perhaps you think that hurting me will help, but is it really going to help – in the long term?'

Now his expression had turned to a sneer.

'Ah, we're back in therapy,' he said. 'Are you going to produce flash cards?'

'No, I'm trying to understand what I can do to help. Why don't you help me to understand?'

'Well, you could start by answering my question. What did you *think* I meant when you *thought* I'd said, what have you done?'

This was it, she thought. Slowly, deliberately, she walked over to her bed and sat on the edge of it.

Non-threatening posture.

'All right, Neville,' she said, then paused. The silence seemed drawn-out, magnified.

If this was a story, where would it start?

'You were right, in a way, about Joanna,' she began. 'She was - difficult. When she played with me I understood it was on her terms - I always did what she said. And she never acknowledged me, apart from when we played on the Wild. If anyone accused her of being friends with me she would turn on me, not them, and take the whole class with her. You know what that's like.'

She wasn't looking at him, but she could sense he was listening.

'And she did, quite often, get me into trouble. I don't know why - maybe Maryam was right and it had to do with economics and class. And, well, you know what my mother was like.'

Hannah rubbed the heel of her hand across her cheek. Neville sat down on the computer chair. It creaked in protest at the sudden descent of his weight.

'She was - different. It wasn't acceptable for a woman to be on her own, with a child, even then - people forget that now.' Hannah sighed. 'You know she told me my father had left when I was very young? It was only after she died that I discovered she'd never been married in the first place. Price was her maiden name - she just added the Mrs herself.'

She laughed a little. 'Hard to imagine, isn't it? My mother being so carried away with passion that she had an illegitimate child? Or maybe it wasn't that - maybe it was something else - something I'll never know. I used to wonder about my father, about who he was, but not now, not any more.'

She had lifted her face, but her eyes were closed. She could hear Neville's breathing.

'Anyway, Joanna. We played her games, by her rules. They were great games - she created a whole world for us to live in, out there, on the Wild. But, yes, she made me do things, fetch and carry for her - she would send me into the muddiest places, or hide from me when she knew I was scared to death of being lost. And of the Others. Once, she pushed me off a wall into some stinging nettles.'

Hannah smiled, reflectively.

'Why did I put up with it? Who knows? I needed that world, however dangerous it was - it was full of magic. I was,' her voice faltered a little, 'a different child there, braver, more adventurous. I - was magic too.'

She looked at Neville then. He was leaning forward, resting his arms on the back of the seat.

'You know, once or twice I did get fed up with her. I walked off, but she always came running after me, crying. Really crying. What does that tell you about our friendship? It wasn't just one way - she needed me as well. But she held the key to that world. Sometimes, when she wouldn't play with me, I used to go down on my own, into the Wild, but it wasn't the same. I needed her to make things spark.'

Neville nodded. Hannah looked away from him, closing her eyes again.

'On the day she . . . I—' She had to swallow, start again. 'We were playing the game I talked about – building stepping stones. It was my turn. Joanna sat on the bank giving orders. Then she tested them.'

Hannah took a breath, started again. 'I was annoyed with her that day, really cross. We'd found a wooden palette and she said if I stood on it, and said some magic words, it would float, just like a boat. So I did that, and of course it sank, into the muddy water. The wood split and I scraped my leg, there was slime all over my skirt, I even swallowed some, I think. But worse than that was the fear of the Others – if you went in the water they could get you. So I was really upset – nearly crying. But Joanna couldn't stop laughing. She said I was stupid, for not looking where I was going – I was like that, as a child, naturally clumsy. I just didn't notice things. Then she said I was weird, like my mother, and no one would ever like me.'

Hannah's lips wouldn't form the next words, she had to press them together for a moment.

'I thought of leaving her then, but instead I said I could build her a special bridge, that would take her straight to the magical world.' She shook her head, then looked at Neville. He was staring at her intently. 'I made sure it looked as though it was safe, but even though she was watching me, I managed to drag the rotten pallet under the water, and I put a stone under it, to make it tip.'

She had to pause, lick her lips. Neville said nothing.

'She said I had to go first, but I knew where it would wobble,' she said. 'So I got across. Joanna didn't. She fell in – as I wanted her to – but I didn't know there was a dip under the water just there – where it got deeper.'

She glanced at Neville, almost pleadingly, but his eyes were closed now.

'All I wanted was to see her fall in, for a change, and laugh at her. But then she did fall, and she didn't come back up.'

Neville leaned back, expelling his breath.

'I knew I should go in, try to save her, but I couldn't - I couldn't go in the water, because of the Others - they would have got me. So I ran for help, up that bank - and that was where I bumped into you.'

Now Neville appeared to be staring at the ceiling.

'So when you said, when I *thought* you'd said, what have you done, I thought, somehow, that you *knew*. Those words followed me, haunted me, you might say.'

'Is that why you told the police I'd done it?'

Hannah shook her head vigorously. 'I told you, I never said that. All I said was the *Others* were there. It was my mother who said there were no others, just you. And I . . . I guess I was just happy that the police stopped questioning me. I didn't think any further than that.'

More silence. Neville wasn't looking at her. She couldn't read his expression, or tell what he was thinking. When silence went on too long with any of her clients she would draw attention to it. *What kind of silence is this for you?*

She decided, instead, to take a risk.

'So now you know. We could go on for ever, apportioning blame. Trying to find out the *truth*. The truth is, we can't ever know. You're saying you don't know what happened just before you arrived, when I was alone with Joanna - I don't know what happened just after I left, when you were there.'

Neville's eyes widened. 'What—' he began, but she ploughed on.

'No one knows, right now, what's happening here in this

room. If I was to say you forced your way in, and threatened me or behaved - inappropriately, it would be my word against yours.'

Neville looked appalled. 'Now just a—'

'I won't do that - of course I won't,' she went on quickly. 'I'm just saying there are situations that can't be resolved - no one can win. And I'm sorry,' she went on, looking earnestly at him, nodding. 'I really am. You have every right to be angry. I was, I still am, angry at myself. For years I thought, *I am a bad person, I should have died.* Is that what you want me to say? Because if it is, I will say it. It's what I thought, every day, for years. Sometimes I still think it.'

For the first time she could hear the emotion in her own voice, feel tears threatening. She brushed her eyes quickly, with the heel of her hand. When she spoke again she sounded utterly dispirited.

'So, go on, Neville,' she said. 'Go ahead. Just do whatever it is you came to do.'

Her head drooped. That was it. She had nothing left.

What could he do? He could report her, she supposed, although he would have to tackle the Swiss authorities, since she no longer practised in the UK. And what for? *Failing to fully disclose facts or evidence pertinent to therapeutic practice.* She knew the regulations.

She couldn't speak, and he didn't. But slowly the quality of silence in the room changed. She could hear Neville's breathing again, she wondered whether he was crying. But then he spoke.

'You know what made me come here, in the end?'

Hannah didn't reply.

'Before I came here, I saw something - nothing much, just two girls running across a road. A major road, with four lanes of traffic. One had hold of the other one's hand and was pulling her along. I saw them weaving in and out of all the cars and vans – horns blaring – I held my breath when they disappeared. It was a wet day, but the sun had come out, a brilliant, glaring sun, the road was glittering and I could hardly see. Just for a moment I thought – it was like an optical illusion – I thought it was you and Joanna.'

Hannah didn't look up. She couldn't.

'They made it, somehow, to the other side. And I could tell – I could just see, that it had been one girl's idea – the other girl really didn't want to do it. It reminded me so much of you and Joanna – how she treated you. I used to think, *why does she put up with it? Why doesn't she tell her where to get off?* Because you were better than that, Hannah – you were better than her. I used to think so, anyway. I used to wonder why you would rather be her friend than mine. Because I liked you, Hannah – I really did.'

That's what he'd said before. And again Hannah felt the flow of heat, the squirming feeling that she always felt in response to the idea of someone liking her.

Neville Weir

Don't come near.

Slowly, she raised her eyes to his. There was something, not friendly, but not entirely hostile in his glance.

'I wondered then, what would happen to that little girl?' he said. 'Would she always follow her friend, tagging behind, always doing what she was told? And I thought about you.' He nodded. 'That's when I decided to come. Just to see if it was you, on the programme, as I'd thought. And here you are. Look at you!' he said, with a not-quite smile. 'Who would have thought . . .' His voice trailed away. Then he said, 'I guess there was always something in you that no one could really see.' His

' was hostile now. Hannah felt cold.

'I guess I thought you were a better person,' he said.

Hannah felt almost too drained to respond, but she made herself look at him. 'I'm not a better person,' she said. 'I'm just the person I am.'

Neville nodded, slowly.

'And in about five minutes, I've got to give a lecture,' she said, getting up. 'So if you'll excuse me . . .'

Deliberately, she turned her back on him. He could do anything to her, she was entirely defenceless. All her skin was alert, as if she was expecting a blow, that he would do or say something apocalyptic, as she went through the motions of putting her bag together, gathering her things.

But all that happened was that after a while she heard him getting up, the creak of the seat, his heavy tread, the click of the door as he left.

He'd said nothing, not even *goodbye*, or *I'll see you in the lecture*.

Hannah's knees felt weak, she had to lean against the bed. She wanted to sit down, but there wasn't time. No time to settle herself, sort through her thoughts, check herself in the mirror, her hair, her outfit, or to alter her lecture. She just picked up her notes, and bag, and left the room.

XXIII

'THERE YOU ARE!' Jopi cried, as she entered the lecture theatre. 'I'm so sorry. I intended to come for you – I really did – but I got caught up in so many things!'

As Hannah drew closer, Jopi said, in a lower tone, 'I was worried we might have overwhelmed you, in the forum!'

'Oh,' Hannah said. 'No.' She managed to smile, avoiding Jopi's embrace.

'See, Isabelle is here!' Jopi said, apparently without noticing. She moved to one side and there was Isabelle, in pale capri trousers, pink heels and a checked shirt, smiling at Hannah.

'Of course I wouldn't miss your lecture,' she said. She stepped forward, and kissed Hannah on either cheek. Hannah managed not to pull away, but she felt brittle, as though she might fall apart at Isabelle's touch.

'Lucy?' she asked.

'Ah, long story,' Isabelle said, pulling an expressive face. 'Some other time, eh? You need to concentrate on your talk!'

'Yes, I think you emailed it to me, Hannah,' Jopi said, bending over the control panel. 'Now where did I—'

Hannah told Jopi not to worry, what she wanted to say had changed now anyway.

'Really?' said Jopi, giving her a searching look. 'So, is there anything you need?'

Hannah extracted a marker pen from her bag. 'Could I have a whiteboard, please?'

François and Michel looked at one another in consternation.

'The interactive whiteboard isn't working,' François ventured. 'Some connection—'

'Don't you have a normal one?' Hannah asked.

'Of course we do,' Jopi said. 'If that's what you want? It's in the storeroom, I think, in the office . . .'

She steered François away, Michel running after them.

'Revolutionary – I love it!' Isabelle laughed. 'I hear you wowed them all earlier,' she said, squeezing Hannah's arm. 'I wish I'd been there!'

Hannah gave Isabelle a brief smile, then she went over to the control panel, and inserted the memory stick. Her hands were trembling, her fingers felt numb, like wood, as she tapped the keys on the keyboard. *I shouldn't have said all that to Neville,* she thought. But she'd had to say something. Her PowerPoint appeared on the screen and she scrolled to the image she wanted, of the human brain. There it was, the cauliflower-like structure she'd spent so much of her life analysing. She tested the mouse, then went back to the lectern, adjusted her glasses, and made herself look over the top of them, into the lecture theatre.

It was full. Hannah had heard the buzz of many people talking from the corridor. There were even more people now than in the forum. Word had evidently got around.

Hannah's gaze flickered along the rows. She saw Heidi, sitting near the front with an older woman. She had turned away, folding her jacket on the back of her seat, but further along the same row Karl nodded and smiled.

Where was Neville? She couldn't see him. Perhaps he wouldn't come.

He would come, of course.

But she had to stop thinking about him. Concentrate on what she was going to say.

What was she going to say?

Suppose he asked her to tell everyone what she'd just told him?

Hannah turned as François and Michel bumped an enormous whiteboard onto the stage and adjusted the stand.

'You're sure that's all you want?' Jopi said.

'Absolutely,' Hannah replied. 'I'll be fine.'

Jopi reached out quickly and pressed her hand. 'A good turnout, eh?' she said, then, lowering her voice confidentially she added, 'I think everyone is on your side.'

What did that even mean?

Hannah said, 'Perhaps we should . . .?' and Jopi said, 'Ah yes – I will introduce you.'

Hannah stood to one side as Jopi took to the lectern, and rapped on it to make the noise subside.

'Now,' she said, 'we come to the best part of this conference. The Grand Finale, as it were – the moment you've all been waiting for . . .'

Everyone fell quiet. As Jopi launched into a summary of her career, her publications, all eyes were on Hannah. She was used to this, of course, yet she felt exposed, as if illuminated by an intense, feral, light. There was that ache in her throat again.

She stared down at her feet. Any moment now, when Jopi finished, she would lift her head and smile.

The door at the back of the lecture theatre clanged open. It was a shock, a sudden jarring. Jopi stopped mid-sentence, everyone turned, Hannah looked up.

Neville.

He lifted his hand in an apologetic gesture, began making his way down the steps. In the silence his footsteps sounded unnaturally loud, heavy, *clump, thump, clump, thump.*

Hannah could feel the muscles in her jaw tightening.

At first she thought there weren't any seats, but then he found one. Right in the middle of the row. Everyone had to move.

'Excuse me, I'm sorry, so sorry.'

As before, the acoustics carried his apologetic murmurings all around the theatre. Then he dropped his bag.

Hannah glanced at Jopi. Her face was inscrutable. As Neville sat, finally, and the rest of the row adjusted themselves she said,

'Well, here we all are – at last.' A low ripple of laughter ran around the room.

'So, without further delay, I present to you our keynote speaker, Professor Hannah Rossier!'

And there was sustained applause.

It continued as Jopi stepped away from the stage and Hannah stood behind the lectern. She looked up and around. *So many eyes.*

Smile.

She cleared her throat and began.

'I made many notes for this lecture. I wrote, and re-wrote them many times. But I'm afraid I've changed my mind entirely, about what I wanted to say.'

Silence. Slowly, deliberately, Hannah's gaze travelled around the lecture theatre.

'What I want to talk about what's happened at this conference.'

XXIV

HANNAH WAS ALONE in her hotel room. It hadn't taken long to pack her bag. Her room had already acquired that empty, transitional feel as though she'd never been there. She checked everything once, twice, then wheeled her bag into the corridor.

Her lecture, and the ensuing questions, had lasted nearly two hours. People had crowded around her on the way out, congratulating her, asking her to give a paper at their conference, or to write an article for some academic journal, sign a book.

Several people had asked her permission to write about what she'd said. Hannah declined, politely, but firmly. She wasn't ready for that yet, she told them.

There was no sign of Neville at the end. He hadn't asked her a single question. Karl had interrupted her while she was signing a book. He'd taken her hand and pressed it 'Fantastisch,' he'd said. Then he said he had to leave early, but he would definitely stay in touch, if she didn't mind, and they had exchanged details.

A buffet lunch had been provided in the bistro, different kinds of salad, wraps, samosas, tiny terrines of Swiss chocolate. Hannah picked at it erratically, engaged by one person after another. She listened to Isabelle talking about Lucy, how they were both trying couples therapy, with Zelie as well, then Heidi interrupted them, her face compressed with fervour.

'That was so good,' she said, and Isabelle agreed enthusiastically. 'You gave us all hope,' Heidi said, then surprised Hannah by stepping forward to embrace her. Hannah moved awkwardly, and instead they kissed on both cheeks. Heidi seemed a little embarrassed but she gave Hannah her card, and said she would email her soon. Then the man with the horn-rimmed glasses approached and talked diffidently, but insistently, about the use of MDMA, or Ecstasy, in memory recall.

Eventually Hannah managed to signal to Jopi, who interrupted them.

'Professor Rossier has to leave,' she said. And she ushered Hannah away, accompanying her to the lift. Hannah felt acutely conscious of what she'd said in the lecture, how it differed from the story she'd told Jopi.

'Jopi, I—' Hannah began, but Jopi pressed a finger to her lips, shaking her head slightly. 'No need,' she said. 'I think you've said what you needed to say.'

Hannah looked at her searchingly. There was something she couldn't quite read in Jopi's face, some distance perhaps, that hadn't been there before? But Jopi spread her arms, 'So, another year, another conference,' she said, sweeping the subject aside.

Hannah tried again, 'I want to thank you—' but Jopi said, 'No, no, I enjoyed it! We should do this again sometime!'

They both laughed. Then Jopi drew Hannah towards her in a firm embrace. 'Take care of yourself, *ma cherie*. Hopefully, you will not need that kind of help again.'

'Hopefully not,' Hannah agreed, disengaging herself. She didn't know whether to say something more, but it seemed the subject was closed. They spoke for a while about the next conference, and payment for this one, then the lift arrived. 'A *bientot,'* Jopi said, *'bonne journée,'* and she'd backed away, her face creased in a smile.

Now Hannah pulled her bag down a single flight of stairs and along the corridor to Neville's room. She hesitated in front of his door, but then knocked, decisively.

There was a pause, then a shuffling sound, then his voice. 'Who is it?'

'Hannah,' she said. There was another pause. She thought she could hear his surprise.

Another bump and the door opened.

He didn't smile.

'Congratulations,' he said, with only minor irony. 'You carried the room.'

'Thank you,' Hannah said, opening her handbag. 'I just thought,' she added, 'if you wanted to talk . . .' She held her card out to him.

'What's this?' he said, without taking it.

'That's my professional email, my mobile number, and, on the back, I've written my address, here, in Switzerland. If you want to talk again, you'll know how to contact me.'

Neville shook his head, laughing a little to himself, before taking the card. 'You mean, if I'm in need of therapy?'

'I mean if you need anything,' she said, coldly. 'You won't have to track me across Europe again. You'll know where I am.'

He inclined his head. 'Well,' he said. 'So.'

His shoulders were bowed as though bearing a weight. He held the card gingerly between finger and thumb.

'Thank you, I guess,' he said finally, and she knew she'd won.

She nodded briefly and turned away.

'Tell me,' he said. 'Do you ever dream about her?'

Hannah paused, without looking back. 'I do,' she said. 'All the time.'

She could sense him watching her as she walked towards the lift.

It *was over*, she thought, as the doors closed on her. *Finally.* Relief surged in her like the Jet d'Eau.

At reception, she handed in her delegates' badge then turned towards the entrance. And there, waiting for her, was Thibaut.

He lifted his arms.

Hannah took one step towards him, then another, faster, she was almost running.

'*Mon coeur,*' he murmured into her hair.

How solid he was, how warm! She breathed him in; the scent of wool, and the unmistakeable tang of cigars. 'You've been smoking!' she accused, pulling away.

'Hardly at all,' he protested. 'Anyway, am I not allowed to miss you?' He drew her back, breathed into her hair. She leaned into him. He was the only person who could hold her like this without making her feel confined.

Even so, she could sense something in him, a subtle withdrawal.

He took her bag from her, wheeling it through the doors, while still holding her arm. 'No, I'm not letting you go again,' he said. 'The car is a little walk away. You might run off, and then I would have to run after you.'

'With your back?' Hannah said. 'You'd never catch up.'

'Ah, but you've been eating all that conference food,' he teased. 'I can see you've put on a few pounds – what?' he said as she elbowed him. They were performing for one another, she thought, and the muscles in her throat began to tense. Thibaut bumped her bag down the steps, then he said, in a different tone, 'Anyway, how did it go?'

'Fine,' she said.

'Ah – that word again – so descriptive!'

'Well?' he said, when she didn't reply. 'What did you talk about?'

'Can we get into the car first?' she said. She needed to leave. The conference had only lasted three days; it felt like months.

She sensed him wanting to speak, then suppressing it.

It took them a little while to locate the car. Thibaut loaded Hannah's luggage into it, and waited until she got in, then manoeuvred himself in more awkwardly, since the space was narrow.

'So?' he said, as she fastened her seatbelt.

'Give me a chance!'

'Another chance?'

'Just start the car. Please!'

Thibaut leaned forward, turned the key in the ignition. Then abruptly he turned it off again.

'No, Hannah,' he said. 'This is not good enough. You've been fending me off for days. First, you leave me a message and I can tell you're distressed, but I can't get through to you. Then, when I do get through you tell me nothing. Nothing! And you won't let me come to you—'

She tried to interrupt him, but he carried on.

'I know this - Neville - has harassed you in some way, upset you, but for whatever reason you *definitely* don't want me to meet him. Why is that?'

All at once, Hannah understood what he was saying. She almost laughed, but something in his eyes made her stop.

'*Well,*' she said. 'I can assure you it's not what you're thinking!'

'What am I thinking, Hannah? Perhaps you can tell me?'

His face was stern, his eyes bleak. She felt a rush of love

for him. She put a hand on his arm, but he recoiled slightly.

'Oh, Thibaut,' she said. It sounded like a sigh. 'You couldn't be more wrong.' She shook her head, emotional suddenly. The temperature in the car seemed to have dropped. After a pause he said,

'The last time we spoke you said you would tell me everything after the conference, remember? But now I see you've changed your mind. You've shut the door on me again.'

'There's nothing to tell.'

'No,' he said. 'I do not believe that.'

'I said I could handle it – and I did.'

'Handle it how, Hannah?' Thibaut said, turning towards her. 'What exactly did you need to handle? You still haven't told me that. Actually you've told me nothing at all. Which is exactly what you always tell me.'

He shifted away from her again. He was so angry. Thibaut was never angry. *This was it*, she thought, and the little pulses in her forehead started drumming. She would have to explain what had happened. But this was Thibaut, the only person with whom she could be who she wanted to be. Already she could feel herself mourning the loss of that person.

'What did he say to you, that upset you so much?'

Hannah closed her eyes briefly. The muscles in her throat tightened further.

'Did you speak to him again, after your lunch?'

'I – no – not exactly. Not until the forum.'

'What forum?'

She hadn't told him about the forum.

She told him then, that Jopi had organised it, but not that she'd done it to protect Hannah, or about the confrontation with Neville afterwards.

'So, you spoke to him in the forum?'

'We both . . .' she trailed off. There were too many gaps in what Thibaut knew. Suddenly they seemed enormous, insurmountable. But she had to fill them in. Controlling her voice carefully, she told him Neville's story, what she'd said about the Others that had led to such terrible consequences for him.

'You didn't tell me this,' Thibaut said.

'I didn't *know*, not until yesterday.'

'So – he blames you – he has held this against you all these years.'

'He did, yes.'

'But not now?'

'I don't think so, no.'

'Because of what you said in the lecture? It must have been good, to have brought about such a change of heart. What did you say, Hannah?'

There was an edge to his voice. She didn't reply. All her earlier elation, the bold impulse that had led to her giving Neville her card, had drained away. Thibaut still didn't know what Neville and everyone else now knew about her.

Thibaut glared out of the windscreen, at the car in front.

'I think there's something you're not telling me, Hannah.'

She could see his face reflected faintly in the windscreen. And beyond that, only cars. So ridiculous to be having this conversation in a car park.

'OK, Hannah,' he said, when she didn't speak. There was such finality in his voice that she put her hand out in terror.

'I will tell you – everything,' she said. 'But can't we just get going – please?'

Thibaut didn't move.

'I promise I'll give you my entire lecture – word for word – I'll talk all the way to Lucerne if you'll just start the car! You drive, I'll talk. Deal?'

For a moment he still didn't move, then he reached forward and turned the key in the ignition.

'There is no deal, Hannah,' he said. 'I need you to be honest with me for once. And then we'll see.'

See what? she thought, but she couldn't bring herself to ask. She leaned back in her seat as the car reversed. The last thing she wanted was to go through her lecture again. And Thibaut didn't want it either – that wasn't what he was asking. But he did have to know what she'd said.

She stared numbly out of the window, trying to remember her lecture, as Thibaut manoeuvred the car out of the car park.

XXV

HUNDREDS OF EYES were watching her, waiting for her to speak. *Blood sport*, Neville had called it.

She'd just said she was going to talk about what had happened at the conference, but she didn't know where to begin.

In the early hours of the morning it had all seemed so clear, as if she'd dreamed the solution. But that was before Neville had come to her room.

Neville. He was there, just a few rows from the front, watching her, waiting to trip her up. She couldn't run the risk of him thinking he still had something over her. She had to say something. She swallowed painfully. Then she said, 'I want to address some of the issues raised by previous speakers – Dr Kruse, Dr Abimbola, and Dr Weir – in their lectures, and in the forum—'

She started to say something else, but her voice disappeared as though she'd swallowed it. It was like one of the nightmares she used to have about lecturing, in which she'd forgotten to get dressed, or lost all her notes.

She looked around the theatre as if she'd only paused for effect. Then, on one side of the room, someone coughed. It was picked up by someone on the other side and continued in the middle, like a staccato theme. It allowed Hannah to wait, to gather her thoughts. In those moments, it occurred to her that she could start with her original lecture, that it was relevant to what she wanted to say. It might, in fact, be the best way to start.

Partly to give herself something to do, she walked towards the whiteboard. There was a marker pen on the little ledge at its base.

She picked it up, unscrewed the cap. Then she pressed the pen firmly to the board, to disguise the tremor in her hand, and wrote:

Thomas Nagel

'In 1974,' she said, 'the philosopher Thomas Nagel wrote an essay called, "What is it Like to be a Bat?"'

She could sense bafflement from the auditorium. *Why was she talking about bats?*

'You will remember Dr Weir's enlightening discussion about octopuses,' she said, before realising that not all of them would have attended his lecture.

No matter. She wasn't going to summarise it now.

'Bats are more closely related to us than octopuses,' she continued, 'but still alien enough to repay investigation. They have very poor vision – they perceive the world primarily by echolocation, but more precisely, in terms of distance, shape, size, texture, than we can by vision or touch. And, of course, they are the only mammals capable of sustained flight. For these, and other reasons, Thomas Nagel said it is not possible for us to imagine the inner life of a bat, if it has one, or how it experiences the world.'

Her original lecture came back to her slowly, like the pieces of a puzzle, and her voice grew stronger.

'The best we can do is to extrapolate from our own experience. We can try to imagine what it would be like to fly out at dusk, navigating by ultrasound, but that is to imagine what it might be like for *us* to be bats. The point Thomas

Nagel was making is that we cannot imagine what it's like for a *bat* to be a bat.'

This led her to what was sometimes called the 'hard problem' by neuroscientists, the relationship between consciousness and the physical body, the brain and the nervous system.

'In order for something to exist,' she said, there must be a boundary between it and the rest of the world. The ability to recognise "self" and "not-self" is at the core of conscious experience. It is also at the core of why we cannot know what it's like to be a bat, or any other creature. We can only know what it's like to be ourselves. We are trapped, in a sense, in our own subjective experience.'

She discussed whether one person's subjective experience could possibly be compared to another's, whether there were any defining characteristics of human subjective experience in general.

'We have a sense of separation and a sense of agency - the sense that we *decide* what we do or do not do,' she said. 'Also, we are able to register our own states of being, whether we are cold, or lonely or hungry. But for the purpose of this lecture, I want to focus on the sense of separation, and the sense of agency or free will.'

'Both of these,' she said, 'are embedded in language. Just by giving us the subjective pronoun "I", language posits a distinction between the self and the rest of the world. In most languages, the "I" is followed by the verb - "I am", "I went", etc, which suggests a sense of agency. So the "I" is active. A sense of responsibility and control is linguistically implied.'

She listed the words that in English imply a sense of responsibility: guilt, remorse, regret, shame.

'We access our memories through language,' she said. 'So

memory presents to us an image of someone who could, and therefore, *should* have more control.'

She paused, too many thoughts jumbling in her head. She thought the energy of attention in the room might have dropped. Was she moving too fast? Too slowly?

'It's important to realise that we cannot access original experience through memory. Our original experiences come to us through the senses, but everything we experience through the senses is altered, and interpreted by the brain.'

The amount of coughing and shuffling in the room had increased. The man with the horn-rimmed glasses was scratching himself, someone else was bending forwards, looking in their bag.

She was losing her audience.

It reminded her vividly of her first experience of lecturing; how determined she'd been, how nearly paralysed by fear. She'd stayed up late doing throat exercises just to make sure she could speak, she'd revised her notes over and over. And on the day itself, she'd managed well enough, she'd thought. At least, she'd got through everything she'd meant to say. But her mentor, who had been observing her, had said in his abrupt way, *Too dry, Hannah – people want stories, not statistics.*

But she hadn't prepared any stories. Sweating lightly, she walked to the whiteboard again.

'Let's put all this into context shall we?' she said, more confidently than she felt. 'Let's create a subjective being of our very own, right here, in this lecture theatre. Let's call her—'

She tried and failed to think of a name that was gender neutral, that worked in all cultural contexts, 'Person A,' she said, writing it on the board.

'Let's give her an age – around thirty. Old enough to be independent but perhaps not very far advanced in her career

– whatever that is. Let's say she's in admin. We can give her a one-bedroomed flat on the outskirts of a city. She probably has to travel into the city to work. Now. Let's take her through her day—'

She wrote, 6 a.m. on the board.

'Person A wakes up. She opens her eyes and a world appears. I say "a world" rather than "the world" because the world Person A perceives is not revealed to her through her senses, but through her brain. So Person A will see the world she *expects* to see.'

'Let's break that down a little.

'What happens when person A opens her eyes? Rods and cones in the retina respond to light waves by generating nerve impulses that are transmitted along the optic nerve to the cortex. But they only respond to a fraction of the electromagnetic spectrum, and they only perceive colour that is not actually present in the world but reflected from it. The curvature of the eye means that light reflected from objects deposits an upside down image on the retina. The brain inverts that image just as it alters all the visual data it receives, adding depth, perspective, scale. There are no rods and cones at all in the centre of the retina, where the optic nerve emerges, but there is no black hole in the centre of person A's vision, because the brain fills it in from memory and context. Similarly, although most of us have two eyes, we don't see two, slightly different images of the world, because the brain creates a single unified vision for us.

'In the same way, it adjusts information from our other senses, such as sound, and motion and balance. Our planet spins on its axis at roughly 1000 miles an hour, hurtling around its star at around 67,000 miles an hour. That star and the entire solar system revolve around the centre of our axy at 514,495 miles an hour. And the galaxy itself rotates, ⸺ all other galaxies, around its galactic centre, at an even greater speed. Yet our conscious perception is not of this frenetic, whirling motion, because our brains grant us a sense of stillness, and balance.'

Hannah turned back to her audience.

'TS Eliot once said, *Humankind cannot bear very much reality.* We are, in fact, perfectly devised to screen out reality. Even a momentary experience of it would be a devastating shock to the system, a sensory overload. The world person A sees is a partial, virtual reality interpreted for her by her brain. If her world didn't appear as she expects it to, how could she function?'

'The world Person A *expects* to see is conditioned by her previous experience, which is in turn conditioned by cultural and political factors. She will remain largely unconscious of these factors that shape her life - she won't see the effects of global capitalism, the supply chain flowing from the third world to the first, the farming practices, chemicals, slaughter, involved in bringing her clothing and food. That is too much information for Person A, who has, after all, to get to work.'

Hannah paused, took a long, slightly shaky, breath. The distance between what she'd said, and what she had to say, seemed enormous. It was like crossing a ravine, blindfold. But the only option was to keep going, take another step.

'All these factors, political, physiological, psychological, environmental, constitute what we might call a *complex causal matrix*, underlying Person A's actions, her thoughts, what she experiences as her choices. One neuroscientist has called it the "darkness of prior causes". I like that term because it suggests a condition of blindness to these prior causes.'

'The condition of blindness affects us in more ways than one. There are some striking examples of attentional blindness on YouTube, for instance, which demonstrate convincingly that we only see what we expect to see. In Person A's case, attentional blindness might prevent her from seeing that her car keys or her glasses were right where she left them. She might put her bag down on a chair and then spend several minutes looking for it, even walking past it several times.'

Thibaut lost his glasses regularly, his pen, his keys. Hannah always found them for him, and he always said he didn't know what he would do without her. But she was getting distracted. She returned to the image of the brain on the screen.

'The cortex, as we know, processes most of its information unconsciously, and we navigate our lives unconsciously, for the most part. In the course of her day, Person A will perform many routine, perfunctory tasks. If asked about them later she will not remember them. But let's say that, on the way home, she is attacked by a man with a knife.'

A minor surge of attention now, like an electric current.

'In that moment she will be suddenly and fully alert. Her body will go into fight or flight mode. Her adrenal glands will release cortisol and adrenalin, her pupils will dilate, her heart rate increase, redirecting blood from her gut to her musculoskeletal system, and rapid breathing will ensure that oxygen is transported rapidly to the necessary sites. This all happens involuntarily, unconsciously.

'But what will her voluntary, or conscious, response be?'

Hannah scrolled to a different slide on her PowerPoint. A series of statements appeared on the screen.

I ran away.

I froze.

I pleaded with him.

I just did everything he told me to. I can never forgive myself for that.

I don't know what came over me – I launched myself at him and fought him off.

'These are all statements from victims of violent crime. They describe responses that were not anticipated by the victims, or planned – they just "happened". Essentially, crisis responses depend on how the body processes the signals from the fight or flight mechanism. They may also partly depend on belief systems. Person A, for instance, may not believe in violence – she may think that the best way to fend off an attack is to conciliate the attacker. However, much witness testimony suggests that people are regularly *surprised* by their responses – they do not behave, in a crisis situation, in the way they think they will, or the way they intend.'

'This has obvious implications for the way we think about free will, or agency.'

Hannah summarised the work of Benjamin Libet, which suggested that all our actions are preceded by impulses from the motor cortex of which we remain unconscious. She outlined more recent research exploring the intricate network of neurons, the changes in brain chemistry that resulted in atypical, sometimes criminal behaviour, and concluded with a quote from the Nobel Prize winner, Francis Crick. "Your joys, sorrows, memories, ambitions, your free will, are no more than the behaviour of a vast assembly of nerve cells."'

'Is that true?' she asked, looking round. 'Do we want it to be true?'

Silence. Hannah's mouth felt dry. She licked her lips. They felt rough.

'We might feel some resistance to that idea,' she continued, 'especially with regard to memory, since so much of our personal identity, our sense of who we are, is stored in our memories. Legal systems also depend on memory – on testimony, for instance, and eyewitness reports. Although we now know that eyewitness reports vary enormously, on hair and eye colour, height, age, clothing, race, and gender. Type of car, and even type of vehicle. The Innocence Project, which began in 1992, has proved hundreds of convicted people innocent by using DNA testing. They say that 63 per cent of wrongful convictions were due to eyewitness testimony. Sixty-three per cent! That's a staggering figure, if you think about it. It suggests we are very poor witnesses to our own experience.

'Memory, as we know, doesn't merely record a situation, it reconstructs it in ways that support our existing beliefs about ourselves and the world. Memory has far more in common with imagination than any other faculty. We don't record information, so much as create it, often creating false memories in the process.'

Silence. Hannah couldn't read it. Was she being too abstract? *Stories, not statistics.*

After a moment's hesitation, she told them about her own false memory, of Danny Millfield, hanging from the ceiling of a room. She hadn't been there, hadn't seen it, yet it now formed part of her bank of memories. It had the power to trigger grief, and guilt.

'It has been proved, many times, that we all experience false memories, especially in states of depression or psychosis. But it's possible to plant false memories into the minds of people with no mental health issues at all. It's now an accepted fact that we can remember things that haven't happened—'

More silence. She had the disconcerting sense that she was talking into a vacuum. The back of the lecture theatre was dark. It helped to focus on that darkness, rather than the faces.

'What conclusions can we draw from this?' she asked. 'What does it all mean?'

'Essentially, it means that subjective experience, which is the only experience we have, our only way of perceiving and evaluating the world, is a combination of misperception, limited sensory input and misleading interpretations of that input, attentional blindness, narrowed focus, imagination, and inferences based on previous subjective experiences.'

'We identify with our bodies when we know next to nothing about them, the extent to which they control us, our conscious thoughts and actions, our unconscious needs, drives and desires. We believe in a continuous, unified self, because our memories grant us that sense of continuity. But memory is demonstrably flawed.

'We believe we are the authors of our own actions, intentions and thoughts, but is that because we simply cannot bear the alternative? We can't think about ourselves without agency any more than we can think ourselves without the linguistic "I" – because we are simply not wired to do so.'

Hannah glanced round for the bottle of water that should have been left for her, without seeing it. She coughed once, then started again.

'What are the implications of all of this for the criminal justice system?

'The Western legal system is founded on the principle of moral responsibility. The idea that criminality is constituted by a guilty *act*, and a guilty *intention*. We know this. What we are less sure about now is where intention comes from.

'Dr Weir mentioned such criminals as Harold Shipman and Luis Garvito in his lecture. There are many others like them. What makes act the way they do? Where does their desire come from? Do they know why they are as they are? Are they responsible for the way they are?

'If they are not responsible, then what can we do about them? Is there a cure for human evil?'

As she said the word 'evil' she had a sudden image of her young client, Lou, and the portrait she'd drawn of Hannah. It made her stumble over her words.

'I – there are things we can do, now, with the human brain. We can recreate parts of it with silicon isomers, for instance. We have already used this technique to correct physical problems – it may be possible in future to apply this technology to cognitive as well as motor functions, to replace parts of the criminal brain using techniques from AI.

'We already know how to use electrical stimuli to alter neuronal activity in the brain. To reduce violent impulses and increase moral awareness. Also, there are significant advances in the use of psychedelic drugs to treat mental health issues such as depression and addiction. They too might be used to treat the criminal mind.

'Is it possible that we could eventually live in a world free from pathology?

'That's a big question, isn't it? Perhaps a bigger one is, would we want to? Or, as Dr Weir put it in his lecture, *do we want to get rid of the difficult octopus?*'

She didn't look at Neville as she said this, but into the dark space at the back of the theatre.

'If I'm not mistaken, Dr Weir was suggesting that it is the darkness, the difficult octopus in all of us, that makes us evolve. Predation, competition, violence.'

Absolute silence from the lecture theatre. Not even a cough.

'But are all these potential "cures" simply ways of treating the symptoms, rather than the cause? Dr Kruse suggested in her excellent lecture that we need to look at the ways in which we, as a society, contribute to criminal behaviour. Should we not also look at the political and cultural contexts of crime that she and Dr Abimbola have spoken about so eloquently?'

There was the noise of someone dropping a book or a bag. It echoed around the theatre, disrupting, yet somehow magnifying the silence.

'So – is there a way forward? What can we do to protect ourselves and our loved ones from criminal behaviour?'

Hannah walked over to the board again.

'In 2017 I attended a conference in London, on Neuropsychoanalysis, where Karl Friston was the main speaker.'

She wrote 'Karl Friston' on the board.

'Karl Friston is, as you will know, a leading authority on brain imaging, and predictive coding. He is also the main proponent of something known as the free-energy principle.

'Much of what was said at this conference was too advanced for me. It involved complex probabilities – advanced mathematics. But I do remember Friston saying that each organism occupies a limited repertoire of states, and is driven to minimise *free energy*, which he equated with uncertainty. About survival, for instance. Most life forms seek to minimise uncertainty about that. Friston said that the brain attempts to anticipate and explain the world for us in order to minimise uncertainty. If he's right, then uncertainty, or the need to minimise it, is at least as powerful a driver as predation.'

She wrote the word 'Uncertainty' on the board.

'As a species, we are not comfortable with uncertainty. We are driven, as the myth of Adam and Eve suggests, to know. All legal systems make decrees, pass judgement, seek to *know* beyond reasonable doubt, that a crime has been committed

and the *intent* to commit a crime was there. But, ir
lecture, I am proposing that there is a value to uncer
or doubt.

'Doubt is creative. It asks *what if?* and seeks different
solutions. It accepts that there are some things we do not
know, and possibly cannot know. If we acknowledge what
neuroscience is telling us about our limited and unreliable per-
ceptions and memories, that thoughts and intentions emerge
from background causes over which we have no control, then
we have to look differently at criminal behaviour. We have
to re-think everything, from the ground up. It would mean a
revolution in law, philosophy, psychology, in every discipline
that considers what it means to be human.

'Science has already driven such revolutions. The
Copernican revolution, for instance, proposed that the earth
went round the sun, which overturned everything that had
previously been thought about the cosmos and about God,
and heaven and hell. And the Darwinian revolution, when
most people accepted our animal ancestry, and our world view
was shaken again.

'Maybe what we now know about neuroscience has the
power to drive another revolution. To *change the narrative*, as
Dr Weir put it. Collectively, for all of us. But especially for
the child in the criminal justice system.'

She was drawing closer now, to the crux of what she had
to say. Even her tongue felt dry.

'Dr Kruse has told us that adolescence is a period of significant neurodevelopment. She said that the child undergoes
dramatic changes as they mature and maturation may not conclude until the mid-twenties. We know about these changes,
not only from neuroscience, but also from research into play.

'In play, children try out multiple identities. They explore

..aries, learn empathy, rules of reciprocity and mutuality. .y has been described as the precursor of language, because it involves complex communications and interactions.

'As children get older, they may be trapped into certain roles at home or school, the naughty one, the responsible one, the one who makes everyone laugh. Internally, resistance to this entrapment, this fixing of identity, can be played out as neurosis, or depression. Perhaps because children lose access to those other selves, those other possibilities. Play provides a way of accessing those other possibilities.

'Through play,' Hannah said, 'the child demonstrates a capacity for change. Which raises the question, if children can change, can they be supported through the changes they undergo? Maybe here, at the interface of neuroscience and psychotherapy, we can find the means to help the child exhibiting problematic or self-destructive behaviour, to stop the cycle of escalating damage Dr Kruse talked about. Rather than criminalising them, from the age of ten.'

At this point, Hannah stopped. She stood back from the lectern, looking firstly at the screen, then the whiteboard, then the clock. Nine minutes to go. She could open the session up to questions, perhaps, but Neville was still there, in the audience, still unappeased. She had to go on.

'N— Dr Weir has described what it was like for him to be criminalised at that age . . . You all know the circumstances – I have said that I was playing with my friend when she drowned—'

Her voice ran out, as though her mind come to the end of a track.

The silence in the room was like an overwhelming pressure, drowning everything out. This was it. The moment she'd dreaded. She could hear her own heart pounding.

Jump! Joanna's voice said.

'But what I told you,' she said, her voice catching on the words, 'wasn't entirely true.'

Fine rain struck the windscreen and the wipers creaked into action. Thibaut should have replaced them months ago. The air in the car had turned oppressive, there was a border of steam encroaching from the margins of the screen.

She'd summarised her lecture for him, briefly. It sounded so different here, in the car. She could sense his resistance, his dissent. Despite his research into drugs that could alter human personality and behaviour, Thibaut had no time for arguments against free will. Hannah had told him it was his Catholic background, and he'd dismissed that as well.

'Not religion, Hannah – life.'

'Your interpretation of it, you mean.'

He'd shaken his head. Compassion, he'd said, could be an act of will. He knew that from personal experience.

The quality of his silence had changed. He was waiting for her to go on, but she couldn't, she had to tell him first, explain what she'd said in the lecture. She moved her hand towards him tentatively, then withdrew it. Her mouth felt very dry.

'There's something I have to tell you,' she said.

A small moan rose from the auditorium as she finished. Hannah didn't look up or around. She waited for it to die down, feeling a combination of terror and relief, a pale green, liquid sensation in her bones.

She'd just told everyone that she'd deliberately placed the stepping stones so that Joanna would fall into the reservoir. Neville couldn't challenge her now. Couldn't stand up, interrupt her, *That's not the story you just told me.*

Everything depended on what she said next.

She couldn't look at Jopi. Or Neville. She looked at her shoes, the dark mules she always wore in lectures. They seemed strange, as though she'd never seen them before. *Whose were they, those shoes, those feet?* A slight sheen on the floor of the lecture theatre swam and blurred in her vision. She glanced abruptly away, towards the control panel, the lectern, the small table behind the lectern. There, finally, she saw the bottle of water that had been left for her on the table. It had been there all the time, but she hadn't seen it. Gratefully, she walked over to it, preternaturally conscious of so many eyes watching her. She unscrewed it with some difficulty, swallowed hard, once, twice. Then she spoke, trying to control the tremor in her voice,

'Was what I did intentional? Yes. I wanted to pay my friend back for the number of times she'd tricked me into falling in. Was I aware of the consequences? No. We've already heard Dr Kruse explain that awareness of implications, and consequences, can take years to develop. That surely complicates the idea of *intent*.

'It's true, however, that my friend died as a result of my actions. And another child suffered greatly, for many years. Although I only learned about that here, at this conference. Attentional blindness, you see,' she said, nodding. 'A deliberate narrowing of focus on myself, in order to survive.

'Do I regret my actions? Yes. Absolutely. Do I feel guilt? Of course I do. Shame? Yes – I have never spoken about it publicly until this conference. I have spent my life trying to rebuild myself into a different person.

'Would I do what I did again? Of course not. Or – at least – the person I am *now* would not do what I did *then* – as a child.

'But that is the question, isn't it?' she said, looking round the theatre. 'What made me do what I did, then? Was it a fully conscious, deliberate act? Where is the line between intention, compulsion, and accident? Can anyone tell me that?'

Silence. Not even a cough. Hannah had the nightmarish sense that her words were stuck in her throat. She could feel herself swaying with the force of what she had to say.

'Obviously, we can't turn the clock back. When I imagine I could have acted differently, it's not unlike imagining I could know what it's like to be a bat. The past is a different country, as someone reminded me only recently.'

She still wasn't looking at Neville.

'Who was I then, in that different country? What was it like for me? Well, I was an only child, raised by a single mother. That fits a certain profile - but we can't say that it definitely gives the propensity to do harm. My mother was a little difficult, perhaps - eccentric, certainly. But she worked hard. And she kept me, at a time when it would have been more socially acceptable to give me up for adoption. That's how it was, for single mothers in Britain back then. She didn't do that.

'I would like to say, here and now, that I do not blame my mother for any of this.

'Nonetheless, as Dr Weir has pointed out, I was a lonely child, on that street of children. I didn't mix well, either there, or at school. Joanna was the only person who would play with me, and then only at certain times, and on her own terms. And only in that particular place.'

Leaves in motion like a fast-flowing river. Shadows pooling on the ground.

'In that place,' she said, too quietly, I could shed myself - and it was so easy to shed, like layers of skin. I could become someone else, some*thing* else . . .'

She cleared her throat, tried again.

'Am I the same person now as I was then? if all the cells of my body have changed, my social identity, my experience, my awareness – how am I the same person?

'If I'm not the same person, what made me change? I could easily have become lost at that time. I could have been trapped on a downward spiral like so many other children. Why was it different for me?

'Jopi was right, earlier, to point out that I had certain abilities that became a platform for me – one I could build on to create a different identity, when my world had crumbled away. Some children don't have that platform. Their gifts, their abilities are different. Maybe the role of the child psychologist, the child psychotherapist, is to help all children build their own platform. And then maybe, just maybe, there wouldn't be so many lost children – children lost to drugs or further crime – or suicide.'

She could see Danny Millfield's legs swaying in the centre of that room.

'The cost would be prohibitive, of course,' she said. 'But perhaps not so great as the costs outlined by Dr Kruse, of putting the child through the criminal justice system, and the ongoing costs of unemployment, and escalating crime.

'The point is, that every child deserves that platform. And we have the capacity to help them build it. By combining neuroscience with therapy, we can help each child to build their own platform, according to their abilities, and their needs. And we owe it to them,' she said, nodding. 'We owe it to the child to accept the contribution we make to each child's darkness. And to accept, that somewhere in that darkness there is value. Something that triggers evolution.

'In my own case,' she said, 'I can say that the darkness in

my life triggered its evolution. I wouldn't be who I am today without it.

'You all know my story now. If I told it differently before, if there are inconsistencies – it's because my memory of that time is uncertain, flawed – because memory *is* flawed. It cannot recreate the truth. The truth of who I was then is lost in that time, that place . . .'

When she closed her eyes, she could see the flicker of light through leaves, the tremble of a shrub as a bird flew out.

'None of this is an excuse for what I did,' she said. 'We all wish that, at certain points in our lives, we'd acted differently, made better, more enlightened choices. But that is *on reflection*, filtered through the lens of memory, and memory, we now know, is the great joker. It presents to us an image of someone who could, and therefore, *should* have had more control. It recreates for us all the factors, all the components and comes up with a different equation. I'm not saying I shouldn't have acted differently, made better choices. I am saying that maybe *choice* wasn't part of the equation.'

Now she could see the Inuit man disappearing into the snow. But there were other, older stories, of men and women who hunted in animal form, wings bursting from ruptured shoulder blades, claws sprouting from the ends of their toes.

Hannah opened her eyes. There was Heidi, next to an older woman Hannah didn't know. Jopi was in front of her, Karl and Isabelle further along the same row. And there, four rows from the front, face shadowy, spectacles glinting, was Neville.

She remembered the feeling in the soles of her feet, scrambling up that bank, the tips of her fingers like claws.

'Maybe there are people out there who still think I should be punished,' she said. 'Joanna's family, perhaps. Or people who simply believe in guilt and punishment and retribution. To them I would ask this question – If they had been in my place – given all the same physiological and environmental circumstances, could they honestly say they would not have acted as I did?'

She was still looking at Neville.

'I have taken some of the blame for what happened on that day,' she said to him. 'I don't know whether it's too much, or not enough. I don't know how much would be enough.

'So now I'm asking all of you,' she said, looking around, raising her voice, 'to tell me – *exactly how much of it I should take?*'

XXVI

A S SHE'D FINISHED her lecture, there had been a
moment of silence, then applause. Some of the delegates
rose, still clapping. She hadn't looked to see whether Neville
was among them. She'd felt a moment of disbelief, changing
to triumph, thrilling through her veins.

Thibaut, however, had made no response at all. Without
looking at him she could sense how his face had changed; how
everything he'd thought about her, all these years, had changed.
They had passed the turn-off for Lausanne, and still Thibaut
had said nothing.

Everything she could think of to say sounded wrong.

Eventually she said, in a small voice, 'Thibaut?'

He didn't reply.

She put her hand out towards his arm, but he shifted it
slightly away from her.

She felt a stab of terror. 'Thibaut – please.'

Nothing.

'Talk to me.'

He half turned towards her then, 'That was it?' he said.
'That was what you couldn't tell me?'

'Yes,' she whispered.

'You could tell a crowded lecture theatre. But not me, your
husband. You couldn't talk to me.'

'I have talked to you—'

'No,' he said, turning away again, 'you haven't. I knew your friend had died, when you were playing together – that was all.'

The tightness in her throat was like a pain.

'All this time,' he went on, as though to himself, 'I assumed you were suffering from some kind of survivor's guilt. Because that was all you told me.'

He turned back to her. 'You couldn't trust me, Hannah, could you?'

'Not you,' she said, 'Me – I couldn't trust myself.'

'But you could trust all those delegates you've never met before.'

'Thibaut – I had to say something – because of Neville.'

'Ah yes, our friend Neville. What did he think of all this?'

'I – don't know – he seemed – I gave him our address. I hope you don't mind?'

'You gave him our address? Did you invite him to dinner?'

'No,' Hannah said. 'I just thought, well, I thought I'd stop hiding, that's all.'

Thibaut said, 'Who are you really hiding from, Hannah?'

Haven't you spent your life hiding, Hannah?

When she didn't answer Thibaut said, 'What did he say?'

'Not much,' she said.

Thibaut shook his head.

'No, really,' said Hannah. 'We barely spoke.'

Thibaut shot her a sidelong glance. 'He must have said something.'

'He asked – if I still dream about her.'

'And do you?'

'Yes.'

'But you wouldn't tell me about that either.'

Hannah closed her eyes. Eventually, she said, 'You're right, of course you are,' but it seemed as though the murmur of the engine, the hum of traffic, had swallowed her words, because

Thibaut didn't reply. She tried again. 'I wouldn't have said anything at all without this conference - not because of you, Thibaut - because of me. I wouldn't even tell myself what had happened!'

She gazed in despair out of the window.

'If Neville hadn't been there I wouldn't - of course I wouldn't - but he was there - and I was - afraid of him - of what he might do.'

She was babbling. Thibaut gave her a sharp, appraising look. 'But you are not afraid of him, now?'

She shook her head.

'*Brava!*' he said, bitterly.

She couldn't speak.

'You think he will contact you?' Thibaut asked.

'I - don't know. That's up to him.'

Thibaut shook his head, laughing to himself. 'You didn't need my help, then.'

'I had to sort it out myself.'

'Yes, of course you did. There is barely any point to me, after all.'

'Thibaut!'

'I have often felt like a bystander in your life, Hannah. Never more so than now.'

'No, Thibaut—'

'I said to myself, give her time, she will open up to you, she will invite you into her inner world as you invited her into yours. But it never happened.'

'That's not—'

'It is true, Hannah! You know it. Do me the honour of acknowledging the truth.'

'I couldn't tell you because I was afraid of losing you.'

'Because - what? You didn't trust me to understand that you

were a child and you acted as a child. Is that what you thought, Hannah? Did you not think that I have also been a child?'

That was it, she thought. A child's game. She saw it through Thibaut's eyes and it was nothing, nothing at all. She needn't have kept it secret all these years, been so afraid. It was as though fear of exposure had become a thing in itself, drawing a noose around her life, around her marriage.

It was over. She'd done too much damage.

Eventually he spoke. 'You know, when I first met you, what I thought?'

Dumbly, she shook her head.

'I thought, there is someone who has been broken, and who has put herself together again. I found that – interesting. Intriguing. I found myself admiring the strength that held you together. Do you remember me taking you to that exhibition of Japanese pottery where all the pieces had cracks or flaws in them – what was it called again?'

'Kintsugi,' Hannah said. She could hardly hear her own voice.

'Kintsugi, yes. I remember thinking, that's like Hannah.'

'Cracked,' she said. 'Flawed.'

'Beautiful, resilient, unique. Maybe I was drawn to that, I don't know. I always liked fixing things. But one thing I have learned, Hannah, in all these years – I can have no part in fixing you.'

Hannah found her voice. 'That's not true,' she said. 'It's never been true.'

'It is true,' he said. He looked at her as if he didn't know her, then turned back to the road.

How would she live without Thibaut?

This would be her real punishment. She shook her head, to dislodge the thought.

'Thibaut, please – talk to me,' she said, after another agonising pause.

'Yes,' he said, without looking round. 'It's not nice when someone shuts you out, is it, Hannah?'

Hannah sank back in her seat. She could think of nothing to say.

She started, then stopped, and started again.

'All the time I've known you, there's never been a single day – not one – when I've not been afraid you would leave, that you would finally see me for what I was, and realise there was nothing to stay for.' Her voice was trembling. 'And I wouldn't blame you if you did, but I can't let you go without saying that you are the best thing that has ever happened to me. I may have been holding myself together before I met you, but for years now, you've been the glue. None of it would have meant anything without you.

'I'm sorry,' she said, into the silence, 'for all the times you've felt shut out. I'm sorry that it took this conference for me to finally come to terms with myself, with what happened. But I've said it now – I've said everything there is to be said. That's it – there isn't any more. No more secrets.'

Nothing.

'Except to say,' she said, her voice breaking, 'that I want – I *need* you to stay with me – to see how things might change now – to give us a chance.'

There was nothing else she could say. She was so tired.

'No more secrets?' Thibaut said, finally. Hannah shook her head. 'That would be a first. I think you would not be my wife without your secrets.'

Her heart pumped a little faster then, as if, without her permission, it had started to hope.

'Ah, Hannah,' Thibaut said in a sigh, and it beat faster

again. Greatly daring, she put out her hand and touched his, on the steering wheel. He didn't respond for a moment, then briefly his fingers closed around hers. Hannah stroked the wrinkled skin of his thumb, the single black hair sprouting from the knuckle. He pressed her hand briefly, then let it go.

There was another long silence, during which Hannah thought of several things to say, and rejected all of them. Finally, Thibaut said, 'I wonder whether he will come to visit us? How will we entertain him if he does?'

'I don't know,' she said, attempting a smile.

'You must have some idea . . .'

'I really don't,' she said, 'I have no ideas left. About anything. I'm exhausted. All I want to do is sleep.'

'Sleep then,' he said, 'I'm driving. Sleep.'

In the mirror she could see his eyes crinkle slightly at her. They looked tired, pouched. Hannah glanced away, afraid of the compassion in them. That willed act.

But she needn't be afraid any more.

Hannah leaned back. The sky was like wet wool. Traffic and buildings flickered by. To one side of the motorway a lake flashed past, alternately silver and brown. She was going home.

Would Neville contact her? She didn't know. She didn't want to know. She wasn't scared of that either. For the first time in her life she wasn't scared.

The rhythm of the car was lulling her to sleep. She allowed the landscape to pulse past without focusing on anything. It moved slowly towards her, then rapidly, past.

She knew that wasn't real, but a visual effect known as motion parallax. Another trick the brain played on the senses. Only the sky didn't alter, one etiolated cloud moving slowly.

Her eyelids drooped, and as she approached the wilderness of sleep she could see again the track between the trees, leading to the reservoir, a jumble of white signs, but no, that wasn't right, the signs hadn't been there then. But she could see the stone bridge and the lily pads, the cloud of flies hovering over the water. She had known the wood was rotten, and slippery. She had put the plank back, anyway. And, as she'd planned, Joanna had fallen in.

She remembered running away, to get help. But then stopping. She'd returned in time to see Joanna's face surfacing, wet hair clinging to it like lank reeds, mouth open. The row of bubbles as she sank again.

She'd watched her rise again, thrashing, and sink a second time, until all that was left of her was a line of bubbles, disappearing into green.

ACKNOWLEDGEMENTS

I DREW ON many and varied resources for this book, including:

Cottis, T., (2021) *How it Feels to be You: Objects, Play and Child Psychotherapy*, London: Karnac

Godfrey-Smith, P., (2016) *Other Minds: The Octopus, the Sea, and the Deep Origins of Consciousness*, London: William Collins

Harris, S., (2012) *Free Will*, New York: Free Press

Nagel, T., *What Is It Like to Be a Bat? The Philosophical Review*, Vol. 83, No. 4 (Oct., 1974), pp. 435–450, Stable URL: http://www.jstor.org/stable/2183914. Accessed: 22 February 2022 10.49 a.m.

O'Keane, V., (2021) *The Rag and Bone Shop: How We Make Memories and Memories Make Us*, London: Allen Lane

Seth, A., (2021) *Being You, A New Science of Consciousness* London: Faber

Solms, M., (2021) *The Hidden Spring: A Journey to the Source of Consciousness*, London: Profile Books

Many people have helped this novel on its journey. I would like to thank my agent, Charles Walker, and my publisher, Christopher Hamilton-Emery, but also the members of my writing group, Cath, Jo and Jenny, for their consistent support and feedback, as well as my other readers, Anna, Bernadette, Ian and Nick, for their time and attention.

This book has been typeset by
SALT PUBLISHING LIMITED
using Neacademia, a font designed by Sergei Egorov
for the Rosetta Type Foundry in the Czech Republic. It
is manufactured using Holmen Book Cream 70gsm, a
Forest Stewardship Council™ certified paper from the
Hallsta Paper Mill in Sweden. It was printed and bound
by Clays Limited in Bungay, Suffolk, Great Britain.

CROMER
GREAT BRITAIN
MMXXIII